What the critics are saying...

About *Jaid Black*

"An emotionally charged, sexual rush... Ms. Black's writing is superb in SINS OF THE FATHER. Her in-depth characters, her hot love scenes and the storyline make [it] hard to put down...definitely not one to be missed."
- *Michelle Gann, The Word on Romance*

"This was my first Jaid Black story but I definitely plan on getting others...Once I picked it up I couldn't put it down. The Possession is a well written, highly erotic story of 2 people who decide to do something different to shake up their lives and find love along the way."
-   *Diane Mason, Sime~Gen, Inc.*
-

"We travel through worlds and cultures, seeing bizarre customs (always related to sex or gender behavior) in each new village. No Mercy was a great story, and a wonderful expansion into the Trek Mi Q'an universe. The sex is hot. Very hot, though there is a plot (and a good one) wending through the story. Again, Jaid Black at her finest."
- *Ann Leveille for The Best Reviews*

Discover for yourself why readers can't get enough of the multiple award-winning publisher Ellora's Cave. Whether you prefer e-books or paperbacks, be sure to visit EC on the web at www.ellorascave.com for an erotic reading experience that will leave you breathless.

www.ellorascave.com

MANACONDA
An Ellora's Cave Publication, May 2004

Ellora's Cave Publishing, Inc.
PO Box 787
Hudson, OH 44236-0787

ISBN #1843609320

ISBN MS Reader (LIT) ISBN # 1-84360-931-2
Other available formats (no ISBNs are assigned):
Adobe (PDF), Rocketbook (RB), Mobipocket (PRC) & HTML

This book is a work of fiction and any resemblance to persons, living or dead, or places, events or locales is purely coincidental. They are productions of the authors' imagination and used fictitiously.

Edited by Heather Osborn, Kari Berton, Martha Punches
Cover art by Darrell King

MANACONDA

SACRED EDEN
Sherri L. King

KNIGHT STALKER
Lora Leigh

DEVILISH DOT
Jaid Black

SACRED EDEN
THE HORDE WARS

Sherri L. King

For Darrell

For adventure and for romance...because we all deserve such things...every last one of us.

'Where there is joy, there is creation. Where there is no joy, there is no creation. Know the nature of joy.' – Upanishads

'The most violent appetites in all creatures are lust and hunger; the first is a perpetual call upon them to propagate their kind, the latter to preserve themselves.' – Joseph Addison

Prologue

Obsidian stroked the silken dip of his wife's naked spine as she slumbered peacefully on her belly in their enormous bed. She was so beautiful that she literally stole his breath. He'd thought her sublime when they'd first met, fighting in the confines of her human home. But it seemed that every day since, he'd discovered something new, something even more incredibly lovely about her.

And she was his. All his. A breathtaking mate and warrior to stand at his side, his perfect match in every way. He couldn't believe his good fortune.

He lowered his hand and stroked the downy soft seam of her bottom.

"Mmmm...," she sighed deeply in her sleep and snuggled deeper into the mattress.

Obsidian smiled and bent his head to kiss her shoulder, nudging the stubborn coverlet, still covering Cady's legs, down about their feet as he did so. The last barrier between his wife's gloriously nude form and his hungry eyes was no more. Cady's caramel-colored skin gleamed in the dim firelight, making him clench his teeth against the urge to ravish her in a wild, animalistic mating. But the time for such wanton play would come later. For now, he would seduce her thoroughly, so that she became liquid need in his arms.

Gently, so as not to wake her fully just yet, he moved to straddle her legs and palm her buttocks in his hands. Her full, rounded lushness overflowed his grasp and he nearly growled with his raging need. He'd always adored her ass.

"Sid," she breathed. Waking, as her own need for him rose with each gentle squeeze his broad hands visited upon her. "Whatter you doin'?" she mumbled, still befuddled with sleep.

"What do you think I'm doing, baby?" he murmured, pressing a heated kiss into the crook of her neck. The scent of her thick braid of hair intoxicated him to the point of madness and he inhaled deeply, unable to fight the temptation. "So sweet," he murmured, and kissed her neck again.

She sighed deeply beneath him, her growing arousal evident as he stroked her. "That feels wonderful," she whispered.

"There is no need to be so quiet, love."

"I don't want to wake the baby." She squirmed beneath him as he delicately probed a finger into the valley of her ass.

"Armand is hardly a baby now," he reminded her. Their son was four years old going on twenty, and as precocious as any Shikar child could—and should—be. But Obsidian knew, no matter how old their child grew, he would always be Cady's baby. She was a wonderful mother, this woman. "And do not worry yourself about waking him. He is with Desondra. She will be watching him for a couple of days...time enough for me to get you pregnant again, I think," he teased wickedly.

Cady woke fully as he moved down and licked the dark crevice of her bottom. "Sid!" she exclaimed with giddy excitement.

"Baby, I love your ass." He slapped her gently and she moaned. He sighed his own contented response. "But that special bliss can come later," he taunted, before flipping her over neatly beneath him.

The golden-orange glow of her eyes gleamed as they roved over him, settling upon the demanding thrust of his heavy erection. "And I thought Christmas was still a few months away," she laughed, reaching for his cock.

Even after nearly five years with this woman, her human ways still gave him pause. It took him a moment to remember this 'Christmas', but when he did, he gave a chuckle. "This present is one to last you the whole year long," he grinned back at her.

"It is definitely long enough to last." She smiled seductively, but the humor was gone from her tone. Her breathing deepened, pupils dilating, lips rosy and full. These signs told him all he needed to know about the state of arousal his mate had reached. But it was not enough. For him, for them both, it was never enough until he was buried balls deep within her dripping channel.

"Spread your legs, baby," he commanded gruffly.

Cady's breath rushed out shakily as she complied. Her nipples stabbed towards the sky, long and thick and hard, and her legs trembled with her aching desire. The wind was cool upon the hot, moist flesh of her cunt, and her clit was tingling and full and begging for his touch.

Settling his weight between her legs, but careful not to give her what she wanted — the full press of his cock — his hands stroked up and over the mound of her stomach.

They burned her with their heat as they moved to cup the fullness of her sensitive breasts, and she could do nothing to contain the moan of pure need that escaped her tight lips.

"I love your nipples. So dark and so long." He moaned hoarsely and dipped his shining onyx head down to taste her.

The full pout of her nipple prodded against his puckered lips. He slurped her in noisily, using his teeth and tongue to bedevil her until she was squirming beneath him with a crazed lust that nearly equaled his own. When she tugged on his hair, yanking hard enough for him to see stars, he chuckled against her and moved to her other tasty nipple. This one he took deep, as far as he could, sucking hard upon the full globe of her breast.

Cady keened wildly and nearly bucked him off with her excitement.

"Patience, love, patience," he crooned around his mouthful of quivering flesh. "I have only just begun."

Cady moaned brokenly and tried her best to prepare for the exquisite torture of her husband's magical hands and mouth.

His teeth bit teasingly into her nipple, tugging on it. He released it suddenly and licked her from the bottom of her breast, up over her nipple, to the rapid rise and fall of her chest. He moved to do the same to the other breast, and the wet trails he left behind only served to make her skin all the more sensitive to each and every breath he tickled over her.

"You're killing me," she sobbed.

Obsidian's teeth were brilliantly white in the dim light as he smiled. "You are such a baby," he teased softly.

Cady punched his shoulder, but he only laughed. His chuckle sent his cock bobbing deliciously against the hot core of her need and she bowed beneath him, seeking him out unabashedly. With a hiss that showed her plainly just how affected he was by all this play, Obsidian jerked away from her.

It was Cady's turn to laugh. "Turnabout is fair play and all that, you know," she giggled.

"Just for that…" He rose, grabbed her ankles and pushed them up around her head. At this angle it was easy for him to bend his head and lay his mouth fully upon her pussy.

Cady screamed.

"So syrupy sweet," he moaned against her. "This is my pussy, baby, all mine. And I am going to play with it all…night…long." He pressed his lips hard against her clit, so that she could feel the firm ridge of his teeth.

She shuddered and tried to lower her legs, but he was far too strong to dissuade from his lustful purpose. The position she was in left everything bare to him, leaving her no secrets, no defenses. As if she'd ever had any where this man was concerned.

From their very first meeting she'd wanted him, just as much as he'd wanted her. Theirs was a match that had been destined from the first. She, who had never really believed in such things as happily-ever-after, was eternally grateful for the bliss she had found with her mate. Sid was everything she'd ever wanted in a man and more. He was her world. Her everything. And always would be. Even if he was the most stubborn thing she'd ever laid eyes on.

Besides herself, of course.

Cady watched, helpless, as the long, silken, black locks of his hair formed a curtain around his head as he buried it between her legs. She felt the fierce burn of his breath as he drew her scent deep into his lungs and back out in a rush. His tongue was liquid fire as it laved her in one long swipe from her clit to her hole and down to her anus.

"*¡Madre mía!*" she screamed, bucking wildly against his face.

"I am going to make you come so hard, baby, you won't see clearly for days," he promised, his lips moving over her as he spoke.

One of his long, graceful fingers probed into her, hooking and seeking for that secret place within her that he knew would push her right over the edge. He found it unerringly, and they both felt the intense contractions of her pussy as the honeyed walls clamped down upon his wriggling finger.

Obsidian let her legs down gently. One finger was replaced with two and he began thrusting his hand into her, impaling her ruthlessly as she quivered and moaned in the onslaught of her release. Deep suctioning sounds echoed in their bedchamber as his fingers moved in and out of her. The noises aroused them both even more. Obsidian thought his shaft would surely burst—it was so hard and full of need. And Cady thought she'd died and found heaven, so intense was her climax.

"I wanted to wait," he growled, spreading her quivering legs wide to accommodate the width of his hips.

"Don't wait," she begged. "I need you now, *please*."

"I am going to fuck you so hard," he moaned as he sank the thick, wide head of his dick into her. "I can't help it. You make me want to ride you until we're both bruised."

His words inflamed her. Her pussy quivered, her breasts tingled, and her nipples, still wet from his kisses and his tongue, felt like stars fluttering on her delicate skin. "Bruise us then. I need you hard and fast too," she gasped.

The thickness of him never ceased to shock her. He stretched her so tight and so full, she thought she might be ripped in two. He was so incredibly big. So breathtakingly huge. His length reached up inside of her to places that were so secret and so hidden, even she hadn't known of their existence, but Sid always seemed to know how to seek them out. How to make her feel so much each time that she feared she might die from sheer sensation.

It was her sacred Eden, here in his arms. Like this. Always so perfect and so right.

Tears filled her eyes and spilled. Obsidian bent to taste them, to capture them with his lips, sipping the manna of her emotion.

"Come on, baby," he crooned softly. His hands stroked the fine, sweaty strands of hair at her brow. "Can you feel me? Can you feel me filling you? Stretching you?" He rocked deeply into her.

"Yes," she breathed unsteadily, wrapping her legs and arms around him to hold him close. "Yes, I can feel you, my love."

"I love you more than life," he vowed, pressing a soft kiss to her lips. For all his earlier, explosive passion, he was as gentle as a summer rain with her now, and it made her heart swell.

"And I you." She gave the vow back to him.

His hips thrust hard into her, the force scooting her upwards beneath him. She gasped and tightened her hold on him as he stunned her with his deep, swift impalement.

Sid rained kisses down upon her face. Tender, gentle kisses to her eyes and her temples and her cheeks. Hard, wet, seeking kisses to her mouth and her neck and her shoulders.

"I want you pregnant," he growled. His lips moved back to hers and his tongue filled her mouth even as his cock filled her pussy. She was burning from her head down to her toes.

Burning…burning…burning…

The smell of acrid smoke filled both their lungs, but neither of them cared. Obsidian pulled back—but only enough to gain more leverage—and began pounding himself into her welcoming body over and over again.

They both felt it at the same time. A release so all-consuming that they could do nothing to stave off the onslaught of it. Cady bit Obsidian's shoulder, screaming around her mouthful of taut skin. Obsidian threw back his head and roared so loudly that the sound echoed off the stone walls of their room. The burning hot scald of his seed flooded her, filling her like a shot that she felt all the way to her heart. Her body tightened, clenched, and gripped his spurting cock so that they both winced with the exquisite agony of it.

Shuddering, sweating, and breathing heavily, they collapsed into the deep down of their bed, holding on to each other for dear life.

After their heartbeats had slowed enough for rational thought, reality intruded, along with the lingering smell of smoke. Looking to the side they realized that—once again—Cady had lost control of her Incinerator abilities. The bed sheets were smoldering. Tiny tendrils of gray smoke and ash flew up into the air, and pinpoints of flickering embers still glowed in the black hole that had been singed into the bed.

They both sighed, thinking the same thing. "Agate is going to be so pissed." Cady winced. "Between me and Cinder, she hardly has time for anything but mending lately."

Unable to contain his mirth, Obsidian chuckled. Cady joined him after but a heartbeat of lingering chagrin at her loss of control. Soon their chuckles turned to guffaws, and then side-splitting laughter. And then all changed to sighs and moans as their love and lust took over once again.

The sheets were forgotten as desire flared as hotly as the gift of fire that lived forever bright in Cady. The knife-edge of lust that was as sharp as the blades that slumbered beneath their Shikar flesh cut them both deep as they mated long into the night.

All was perfect. All was love.

Chapter One

"I think that, for once, I am actually looking forward to this visit to the surface world," Sid admitted to his wife.

"Well, now that the Daemons are reduced to nothing more than a handful of stragglers, I can see why. Without them to worry about, it'll be a field trip for us instead of a battle," Cady chuckled.

"This is true. But long before the Daemons began escaping into the world of humans, it was rare that I had any true interest in visiting there."

"But that was before you had me to take you to all the fun and happening places up there," Cady teased, buckling her *Sig-Sauer* 9mm P-226 pistol to her black-clad thigh. Though she didn't expect any danger tonight—it had been almost a year since the last Daemon attack after all—it never hurt to be prepared. The long skirt of her reverend-style overcoat would hide any evidence of the weapon should she garner too many curious stares...she hoped. But no way was she leaving her new favorite weapon behind.

"Baby," he chided, "I have my doubts that you even know of one such place. Before you became one of us, all your days and nights were spent working and fighting Daemons. You had no time for such idle pursuits as fun."

"Ooh, that was cold. I should spank you for that one," Cady mock-pouted, knowing that his words were true.

"Not before I spank you first," he quipped back with an exaggerated leer.

Pulling his long, black hair into a ponytail at his nape and securing it with a strip of rawhide, Sid strode over to an intricately carved wooden side-table that stood by the door.

Cady couldn't help but admire the play of his roped muscles beneath the tight material of his black clothing. His tight, black, sexy clothing.

Tonight they wore no armor, as they might have but a year before when evil Daemons ran rampant over the earth. But they both preferred wearing dark colors so as to blend in with the night as they roamed above. Old habits died hard, it seemed, despite the lack of danger.

And they *had* to roam at night after all—Shikars were ultra-sensitive to the sunlight. Their race had dwelled in darkness for so long—thousands of years—that tolerance for the bright rays of daylight had been bred right out of them And though Cady had once been human herself—turned Shikar only by the powerful magic in the semen of her husband—she had not yet tested the theory that she might still be able to walk in the light.

She wasn't afraid of the risk, not really. But Obsidian had forbidden her to even think of testing the resilience of her flesh in the rays of the sun. While she wasn't always inclined to willingly heed a command that her beloved—yet arrogant—husband gave her, she had seen the stark fear in his eyes as he worried over the possibility of her injury, or even death. So she had, for once, decided to let her dearest have his way.

Giving up the sun was such a small price to pay for this new life she'd gained. A loving husband, a perfect son, the power to create fire with her mind and her will, and the ability to shoot deadly, poisonous blades from her flesh—without any real pain or effort—were huge boons that made the loss of daylight seem almost insignificant in comparison.

"I almost forgot, Desondra brought this when she came for Armand." Sid's deep, sexy voice snapped Cady out of her wandering thoughts.

She reached for the piece of folded parchment he held out for her. "Ah." She nodded when she realized what it was. "I'd meant to ask you about this earlier."

It was the main reason they were going up to the surface world, this piece of parchment. Or rather, what was written on it.

"Let's see…Edge wants some peaches, Emily wants some new handcuffs—how the heck am I going to find 'official police handcuffs'? Steffy wants some hot dogs and the new *Hooverphonic* cd, Cinder wants some clove cigarettes and," she paused, incredulous, "a DVD of *The Three Stooges*. You gotta be kidding me. No wonder the generators keep running out of fuel…Steffy and Cinder are hooking up goodness knows how many devices to 'em."

Sid only chuckled and buckled up his knee-high, oxblood boots.

"Where was I? Hmm…Desondra wants chocolate, Agate wants—oh lord—*fuck-me-pumps*!" Cady laughed over that last request on the list. She looked up at Sid, whose Shikar-yellow eyes were wide with avid curiosity over such a request. "She actually wrote 'fuck-me-pumps' on here. The woman never ceases to surprise me."

"I can only imagine where—or from whom—she learned of those," Sid rolled his eyes comically. "Grimm bless her, she is always looking for something new to inspire her designs." Both Sid and Cady had, on numerous occasions, taken great joy in testing out those designs.

"Yes. Our own resident sex toy and lingerie designer, dear Agate. I just know she's going to drive one lucky man crazy someday. I'll bet you anything, once she's found her mate, she'll constantly want to use him for 'research'." Cady's laughter subsided into chuckles.

"If only all warriors could be blessed with a woman so seriously devoted to the joys of physical pleasure." Sid leered wickedly at her.

Cady stuck her tongue out at him cheekily before folding up the list and tucking it into a pocket at her hip. "Well, are we ready to go?"

"Let's get this party on the road."

Cady laughed. "You said that all wrong. You should've said, 'let's get this party started', or 'let's get this show on the road'. One of these days, Sid, I'm going to have you using slang properly, like any other American."

"I use these 'slangs' plenty, but only when you are conveniently absent." He tugged playfully on her long, dark braid.

"Jerk," she snorted. But she couldn't contain the warmth she knew was flooding her eyes. Goodness, but he was a handsome devil—even when he was teasing her so mercilessly.

"Yes, but I am *your* jerk, and that makes it all better." He winked at her and took her hand. "Hold on, love," he murmured, and the world disappeared.

When the darkness of nothing flared back into the light of substance they were standing in a wooded thicket of pine trees. Cady immediately recognized the terrain as that of the lands surrounding her former home. She had planned to come here tonight, before moving on to the nearest town in which she felt sure she wouldn't be recognized, but now…she wasn't certain why she'd wanted to come and see this place again. It brought with it such painful memories, this old home of hers.

The very same home that the Daemons had burned down…but that violence was done, and she hardly dwelled on the loss of the home in which her grandparents had raised her. Not anymore. She had a new family now, a new life as a Shikar warrior…but there was a suspicious pang in the vicinity of her heart as she looked about her at the land that was at once familiar, and yet so very strange now that she was no longer a part of it.

She hadn't expected to feel so strongly about this place…even after so long a time as five years. But then, time to a Shikar—as she was now—was reckoned differently than time to a human. Shikars lived such very long lives. Five years had passed by so quickly for her, more quickly than she had realized before coming here tonight, and all the pain and loneliness she'd experienced in this place still seemed fresh and raw in her heart.

"You miss this place, despite your unsavory memories." As always, Sid seemed easily capable of reading her thoughts. "And it pains you."

"Sometimes," she admitted, drawing closer to him. "But never so much as now that I'm actually standing here in person. I wanted to come and see it so badly…"

"This is the only real visit you have had here since becoming one of us. Perhaps now that the wars are over we can visit more often—"

"No." Cady stopped him, turning and placing a soft hand upon his mouth. She looked deeply into his eyes—those glowing eyes she loved so much, since she'd first seen them shining out from the dark shadows of her living room—feeling her aching memories subside and fill with the warmth of his presence. She lowered her hand and rested it upon the steady, reassuring beat of his heart. "No. This place isn't my home anymore. It hasn't been for a long, long time. Even before you came for me…I wasn't a part of this land. I'm not sure I ever really was."

"You have always been a warrior. That kept you apart from other humans, through no fault of your own. From the moment you saw Daemons killing your parents and brother, your life changed irrevocably into a mad race of fighting and survival. But that is not so terrible or lonely an existence now, is it? Now that you belong to us, to our world? Now that you know and understand your strength and power? Now that you are not so alone?"

"Everything is perfect, and will always be perfect, so long as you're with me," she said at length, and meant every word of it.

Sid grunted, but despite the show of his seemingly endless male arrogance, Cady knew he was very pleased with her answer.

"And what about you?" she asked. Broaching a subject she hadn't dared to in the past few months for fear of upsetting her love.

"What *about* me?" he returned. Stubbornly feigning ignorance, even though he knew full well what she meant.

Cady twisted her lips and trudged on. "How is it for you now that the Horde wars are pretty much over? You've been fighting your whole life, born into the war that your parents and their parents before them were born into. Now that it's over, what will you do?"

There was a hunted look in his eyes then, a second and no more, before he masked that all-too-telling reaction to her words. He didn't want to talk about it, it was clear by the look in his eyes. But Cady knew now what she'd been fearing for months—that Sid was indeed cut adrift, almost without purpose since the fighting had ended. He was a warrior through and through and it was in his will and in his blood to fight. To triumph over their enemies, the evil and hated Daemons. Now there was no great war to wage, no battles to engage…nothing that was familiar to him.

How could he stand it? And she, fighting the same foes since she'd turned sixteen, how would she cope now? How could either of them survive this time of…peace?

How could any of the Shikar warriors learn to live a life that no longer involved such danger and death, now that a centuries-old war was finally ending?

"I do not wish to think on such dark thoughts now," he said flatly.

"We need to talk about it soon, Sid. You can't just ignore this. Now that you aren't fighting every hour of every night, you need to think about where to direct your gifts as a leader of men."

"I know what you are insinuating, my love. But I will not join the Council. Only the older warriors, who have finished with their battles, belong on the Council."

Cady sighed. "That's the way things used to be. But everything has changed now. The Council will need young men like you to lead the Shikar race into a new era—"

"There are still a few battles yet to fight. It may have been almost a year since a Daemon strike, but there are still some stragglers left wandering—you can trust in that. We'll decide what to do when *all* the Daemons have been exterminated—all of us. Cinder and Steffy, Edge and Emily—we are still a team, and we need to decide what to do as a team."

"I know that, Sid." She answered as patiently as she could—which wasn't very much...she wasn't known for her patience, after all. "But you need to give all this some thought before going to them. You are their leader—they'll look to you for guidance above all things. You need to have some idea of where to go in the end."

"*Bah.* Let us forget this sightseeing business and get our shopping done, woman," he said, in desperate effort to drop the subject. He grabbed her hand once more and tugged her along behind him. She was a small woman—barely over five feet tall, compared to his nearly seven foot height—and it was all she could do to keep up with his long-legged strides as they trudged through the shadowy forest towards the town.

"Sid, slow down." She grunted as she stubbed her booted toe on a jutting rock. "We can't go into Lula, someone is bound to recognize me."

He stopped so abruptly that she slammed into him. It was only his quick reflexes that kept her from falling as he reached out and held her steady. "I forgot," he admitted with a chagrined flash of blazing white teeth.

"Well, go on then," she said, softening her tone, knowing he was still unsettled by their conversation. "Travel us there."

"Are you sure you want to visit Gainesville? I could take you anywhere, you realize. Paris, Los Angeles, Melbourne— anywhere you want to go."

"Yes, but the only place I can get good—really good—dark roast coffee is at the Coffee Shop of Horrors in Gainesville. And I need that coffee, Sid. I mean I really, *really* need it," she warned.

"Yes, of course. I know that, baby," he soothed her. In fact, he knew better than anyone just how *much* she needed that boost of energy in the early hours when their energetic son woke them from their slumbers. Cady wasn't a morning person in the best of circumstances, but the coffee definitely helped. He wasn't about to come between her and her bean-juice fix.

"And I know where everything is in Gainesville, or I used to. I grew up around that city. Everything but Emily's handcuffs should be easy enough to come by there, even Squaker's senior formula cat food." Squaker was her beloved cat, older now and living in the world of the Shikars, but still very picky about his brand of grub, and Cady wasn't about to disappoint him.

"Then Gainesville it will be, my love." Sid took her hand, brought it to his mouth for a kiss, and they Traveled for the second time that evening. And though the world disappeared around them, they held on to each other so tightly, not even an army could have separated them.

Chapter Two

"*Sid, put that down,*" Cady hissed.

"I can think of many uses for this," he mused, fingering the long, leather whip almost lovingly.

"Think all you want, but we ain't gonna buy it."

"I think we should," he insisted, piling the now coiled length of the whip onto the two shoeboxes he already held.

"Well I *don't* think we should," Cady gritted.

A look of stubborn determination filled his eyes and twisted his lips. He looked ready to do battle over the damn whip. "We *are* going to purchase this."

Cady let out a whoosh of air and tried a different tactic. She let her eyes soften as she sidled closer to his side in the aisle of the only sex-toy shop in the city. "We came here for Agate's sex shoes and I just don't think we can carry all this extra stuff you keep piling on."

"I only purchased Squaker a few extra toys—"

"*Seven* extra toys."

Sid glared at her for interrupting. "And a couple of boxes of Godiva chocolates for us to share, and a stun baton. That's all."

Cady almost smiled at his mention of the stun baton—she'd wanted one of those for a while now. "Alright, we can buy the damn whip. But no way is it gonna find it's way into our bedroom, buddy."

He frowned. "I would never hurt you with it." He drew closer to her and lowered his voice into that soothing, magical tone that she always succumbed to in her moments of weakness. "I would make you scream...but only with pleasure." He leaned in so that his breath tickled her ear. "Pure...unadulterated pleasure."

Cady shivered. "Okay," she said shakily, "we're definitely buying the whip."

Sid drew back, smiled into her eyes, and moved on to an aisle full of flavored lubricants, leaving her to stare dazedly after him.

"How the hell does he *do* that," she muttered under her breath, before tagging along after him.

"This strawberry oil will heat when you blow upon it," Sid declared, brandishing the jar like a trophy.

Cady hated herself for blushing when the store's clerk looked up and winked at her. If Sid had caught such a forward thing from another man...well, at least he could Travel them out of there if the cops dropped by.

"*Hush*, Sid," she growled, drawing up next to him so that he could better hear her lowered voice. Not that he wouldn't have heard it anyway. He was a Shikar, and all Shikars had exceptional hearing. Sid probably could have heard her loud and clear if she'd whispered to him from the farthest corner of the room. "Keep it down, will you?"

He only grinned.

Cady gritted her teeth.

"Do we have enough monies for five of these jars? They come in so many flavors, I cannot choose just one."

"Honey," Cady rolled her eyes, "it's not a matter of money. Tryton supplied us all with plenty of dough before he took off for his sabbatical. It's more a matter of how many parcels we can carry with us back to the park, where we can blip out unseen."

"I think I can carry one more bag," he said with affronted dignity.

"I'm not saying you can't, but can you balance it with the dozen or more others we've already got? It's not a matter of strength here, but a matter of balance."

Obsidian snorted. "I've been shopping with you before, woman. I understand the mechanics of the sport."

Cady almost laughed, but managed to choke it back in time. It wouldn't do to give in to him so easily again...after all, he'd denied her the sniper rifle she'd so wanted back at the hunting supply store. "Just pick one flavor and have done with it. I'm ready to go back home and..." She paused for effect before she played her trump card, a trick she knew would make him putty in her hands for the rest of the trip, "*snuggle.*"

He visibly stilled. The bright glow of his eyes intensified, and Cady could plainly see the insistent rise of his shaft beneath the covering of his pants.

"We're going," he snatched the jar of strawberry oil, piled it on with the rest of his purchases, and strode purposefully up to the checkout counter at the front of the shop. He looked back at her with a blazing hot gaze as the man behind the counter rung up their items. "Well come on, love, we haven't got all night," he commanded impatiently.

Men, Cady thought. Shikar or human, when it all came right down to it, they were the same.

Sid's black trousers did very little to hide his growing desire, and the ever-growing heat in his gaze was all the warning she received. His long, nearly waist length hair whipped about him, so quickly did he snap his attention back to the shop's clerk.

"Where are your bathing room facilities?"

Cady felt faint.

"Wha-huh?" The clerk asked in obvious confusion.

"The bath, where is the bath?" Sid was clearly growing more and more impatient with each second that passed.

"You mean the bathroom?"

"Yes, yes of course. Where is it?"

"We don't have a bathroom for public use. You'll have to go to the gas station across the street."

Sid reached forward just as Cady moved to get a handle on a situation she knew could easily spiral out of control. Her hand fell on his arm as his hand latched onto the collar of the poor, unsuspecting man's shirt.

"Tell me where your bathroom is or I'll beat the information—"

"What he means to say, sir," Cady desperately tried to diffuse the situation, "Is that we'll pay you three hundred bucks if you let us use the bathroom for, say, twenty minutes."

Sid released the man, who stepped back with mixed look of relief, incredulity, and suspicion.

"You gonna mess anything up in there?"

"No, sir," Cady hurriedly assured him, doing her best to ignore the warm hand of her husband as it fell upon her backside caressingly. "In fact, we'll pay you five hundred dollars—and you'd better make that thirty minutes," she blushed, from embarrassment as much as arousal, knowing the clerk—unless he was unbearably dense—must have some idea by now of what they intended.

It had to be doubly obvious, when Sid bent low and licked the corner of her mouth—he'd apparently already forgotten his displeasure with the clerk. His mind was on other, headier things. Much more *pressing* things, from the look of the full, heavy cock tenting his britches so demandingly.

The man grinned lasciviously, and Cady eased, knowing everything would be alright in just a few moments. "The bathroom's in the back."

Cady quickly handed him the money for their purchases, plus the five hundred she'd promised him.

"If ya'll mess anything up, I'm calling the cops," the man warned, fingering the wad of twenties Cady handed to him.

"I wouldn't expect less of you," Sid replied stonily, already pressing Cady towards the back of the store. "You will, of course, guard our bags while we are making use of the facilities?"

"Sure, no problem," the man stared with blatant curiosity after them, until the closing of the bathroom door sealed them off from his gaze.

"Drop your leggings and bend over," Sid commanded the very moment the door latched shut behind them.

"Oh baby, I fucking *love it* when you're impulsive like this," Cady panted, more than eager to comply with this particular order given her.

"You asked for this, taunting me so shamelessly. Hurry." His hands were none too steady as he unfastened his own pants.

Cady felt giddy with excitement. Hooking her fingers into the waistband of her trousers, she quickly peeled them down to her ankles. But before she could turn away and do as he had commanded, Sid swooped down for a long, deep, soul-searching kiss.

His lips were like fire. His tongue like wet, molten lava in her mouth. She was seared from head to toe with a violent eruption of need and desire.

Long moments later, when they were both completely out of breath, Sid tore himself away and turned her around forcibly, almost too roughly, and pressed her forward over the white porcelain of the bathroom's sink. Luckily, the room was well tended and far cleaner than the seedy hotel room they'd used during their last visit to the surface world.

"I can smell your heat," Sid growled in her ear before biting at it playfully.

"*Shhh*! That guy's probably listening at the keyhole right now." But despite her warning, she moaned softly with her own considerable need.

"Let him listen." Sid's fingers probed her slick folds, so exposed to him in this position that it was easy for him to feel her syrupy arousal, proof of her desperate need of him. "It will only heighten our experience."

And it would. They both had a seriously voyeuristic streak, loving the threat of exposure, and the risk of having eyes watching their every move as they mated. It was a spicy stimulant, one they frequently indulged in, given the right circumstances.

"I *have* to lick this sweet pussy of yours," Sid breathed heavily, squatting down behind her, spreading her wide for his pleasure. "It's so damn tasty. I could eat you out for hours."

"You have several times before," she panted.

"Not this time. Only a little taste of your honey for now. This time is for hard, wet fucking."

"Quit using that tongue of yours for talking, you tease, and go down on me. Lick and suck my pussy until I come all over your mouth."

Sid physically lifted her higher, positioning her soaking cunt over his mouth. His breath nearly burned her alive. "You tease me too much sometimes, my love," he murmured. "This time, you'll get exactly what you deserve."

Any retort she might have made was lost when his tongue darted out to lap at her hot juices. His face was buried completely between her legs. And it wasn't only his tongue that devilishly tormented her, but his lips and his teeth too. Her pussy throbbed and burned with desire. Her bottom tingled where his hands held her so tightly, lifting her as he rooted and sucked and licked and bit her.

She nearly screamed when his face burrowed deeper, her pussy and her anus completely open and loved by his hungry mouth. "Stop, Sid. Stop," she panted.

Her pleas went unheeded. His fingers dug harder into her, his lips and teeth latching onto her clit until she moaned.

"Sid, please. I need your cock. Please, your cock, *now*," she rambled, intoxicated and nearly mindless with her intense need to be joined with him.

His tongue flickered over her clit one last time before releasing her. "I'm going to fill you so deep and so hard that you'll be feeling me inside of you for days."

"I can already feel you," she cried.

"You're so wet. My face is drenched with your sweetness and your body's exquisite perfume. I love how responsive you are, how ripe and ready you are for me."

"Take me, Sid. Quit teasing! I need your dick inside me."

His fingers came around her face to probe at her trembling lips. "Suck on them. Taste yourself as I taste you."

Cady eagerly took two of his fingers deep into her mouth. Licking and laving them, sucking and biting them, in a way she knew would make him crazy.

His wide, mushroom-headed shaft slid into the wetness of her folds. Sid unerringly guided himself into her, stretching her without entering her, driving her wild with anticipation. "Hang on tight." His free arm came around her, his hand covering one of hers as it gripped desperately onto the rim of the sink.

His cock slammed home, lifting Cady up off her feet with the sheer power of his thrust.

Tears burned her eyes with the delicious pain of his deep, hard penetration. She moaned, pressing back even tighter into the cradle of his hips, biting onto his fingers.

"Are your nipples hard, my love?" His magical voice rumbled in her ear. He was using all of his Shikar tricks against her. The power in his voice made her already hard nipples swell and elongate even further beneath her clothing. Her breasts felt heavy and full, more now than before. Her entire body flushed and tingled. She trembled from head to toe...and all the while, his cock rested deep inside of her, stretching her to the breaking point.

Obsidian's breath thundered at her ear.

Cady twisted her head, releasing his fingers. "Stop tormenting me." Her words shook with the force of her need.

"We torment each other," he rasped. He pulled almost all the way out of her, waited just long enough for her to keen at the loss, and then slammed back into her. His fingers, wet from her mouth, moved now to cup her mound and rhythmically massage her clit.

"Sometimes I want to take you so hard that we become one being." He pressed a hot kiss against the sweat-moistened tendrils of hair at her temple.

His words never ceased to inflame her pleasure.

"And sometimes…" He slid his long, thick cock out slowly and then gently back in to her heated core. "Sometimes, I want to make it soft and sweet and last for so long that we both dissolve into pools of warm, liquid light."

"Oh *god…*"

"Our thirty minutes are almost up," he panted. "Time is growing short…"

"Then hurry. Slam me. Fuck me. Slam me hard, *Sid, please*," she cried.

"Anything my lady wishes," he growled fiercely. Both their bodies shook with the force of his thrusts as he moved, pistoning in and out of her welcoming heat, catching her up in a whirlwind of excitement that made her head swim and her breasts bounce.

"I love you, I love you, *IloveyouIloveyou*," she chanted like a mantra.

"And I love you more," he said softly at her ear, pressing kisses all over her neck and the side of her face. His fingers expertly plucked at her clit. He rotated his hips against her in a way that she loved, making her see stars behind her tightly shut eyelids.

"I'm coming," she panted on a shallow breath. "Oh god, oh fuck, I'm coming."

"I'll be there with you," he vowed, tightening his arms around her and nuzzling her neck.

In fact, he was there a scant second before she, the hot wash of his release flooding her to her core. Her scream would have echoed audibly out into the store, but Sid had enough presence of mind to bring his hand down over her mouth to stifle the desperate cry. Her body clamped down like a vise, trapping them both together in a deep, hard embrace of stunning release.

It was actually thirty-seven minutes before they emerged from the bathroom, but the overly flushed store clerk and two wide-eyed customers didn't seem to mind that at all.

* * * * *

"I told you it would be a pain in the ass to drag these bags all the way out here."

"No one likes a braggart, baby." Sid's armload of boxes and bags teetered precariously with each step they took.

It didn't help matters that the both of them still suffered from weak knees and giddy heads after their steamy visit into the sex-toy shop's bathroom.

"We really need to buy a van or something for these excursions."

"There is no way in the Christians' hell that I am going to let you drive me anywhere." Sid's panicked shudder nearly toppled his mountain of packages.

Cady halted, incredulous. "What! Well fuck you, buddy! You've never even been in a car while I'm driving, how would you know anything about the way I drive?"

"I do not have to experience such a thing, to know exactly how it will be. You are a wild woman in everything you do, from fighting to fucking and everything in between. I have a hard enough time getting in a car with Cinder, who is a very careful driver now that Steffy has taught him all she knows. You, I know, would have us slinging all over the place at a velocity to rival even a Horde Canker-Worm—I know it. You simply cannot do things in half measures. It is against your very nature."

"You are so full of shit, Sid," Cady huffed, growing more and more irritated with his assessment of her character. "I thought you liked the way that I do things. Especially love-making—I've certainly never heard you complain about it—"

"Now, baby, I am not saying your wild ways are a bad thing. That is not what I meant." He immediately backtracked.

"Don't take that tone with me," she barked. "I'll have you know that I'm a very good driver. I've never had an accident or even come close. So I've had a few speeding tickets, that's not a big deal—"

"Ah ha!" Sid immediately latched on to her last statement, as she should have known he would. "So you *do* drive fast. See? I do know you, and therefore I know exactly what to expect if I ever allow you to drive."

"*Arrgh*! As if you could ever *allow*, or disallow, me to do anything. I make my own decisions!"

Sid winced. "I know that, of course I do. But please, baby, I am asking you for the sake of my sanity, do *not* ask Tryton for your own vehicle. I just don't have the courage or the stomach to handle being in a small, steel machine, hurtling through the lands with breakneck speed."

"I don't need to ask Tryton for a car. I can buy my own," she persisted stubbornly.

"Please, baby. I'm begging you. Please."

"Oh, all right," she conceded grumpily. Her arms were too tired from carrying all her packages to continue the argument just now anyway. "I'll *think* about it," she added, just to ensure that she had the last word.

Sid only exhaled a long, relieved breath and trudged along beside her.

A silent truce lasted for several minutes as they made their way through the sparsely populated residential area, which lay just outside the secluded park to which they were headed. Not so much a park, as a small clearing amidst a thick copse of maple, oak and pine trees, the area was shadowy and secluded enough for them to Travel without any risk of being seen.

At one time the small park might have been used as a family burial plot. But that had been so long ago, that the half dozen or so grave markers of stone and wood were smooth and covered with lichen. The ravages of time had also piled soil on top of the graves, so that most of the markers were also crooked or half covered with earth.

Cady had always liked the quiet, secluded spot. As a teenager, with the long-anticipated privilege and freedom of a vehicle to drive, she'd lingered here for hours — on those few days when she didn't have to leave school and head straight for a martial arts class or the shooting range. Sitting amidst the tall weeds and grasses, she'd spent rare lazy afternoons wondering about the great mysteries of the world and her place within it. The eerie ambiance of the place had appealed to her on many levels, and the silence and the stillness were so very different from the constant ravaging pace she'd set for herself in life.

She wondered now how her life would have been if it hadn't been for the death of her family at the hands of the Daemons. On one hand, if her family had lived, she would have had a much more normal life, filled with all the love and laughter and safety of her younger years. On the other, she would never have known of the existence of the Daemons, would never have had the opportunity to hone her mind and body into a weapon to fight against their evil threat. And she certainly wouldn't have met her husband or any of the other Shikars whom she now regarded as friends and family. And, perhaps the most important thing — aside from meeting Sid — was that her son, Armand, would have never been born.

It served her no purpose to think on such things. Only aggravation and upset. But this was not the first time she'd dwelled on what might have been — on what could have been — and it would probably not be the last time she did so. Cady was so grateful for the happiness she'd gained in life. Happy beyond measure with her place as a warrior and a mate and a mother. But she was saddened still for all the losses, too.

A part of her would always feel such sadness. She knew this. It was her fate and it could not be undone. But still...she could wonder. And she could wish. For such was the part of her that was still human and would never change, no matter how strong the practical, fatalistic Shikar blood that flowed in her veins.

She was still as much a human as she'd ever been—in her heart and in her soul. Thankfully, her beloved Obsidian knew and understood this. It was only one of the million or so reasons why she loved him as deeply and passionately as she did.

No matter what might have been...she knew for a certainty that she belonged with Obsidian. He was the perfect mate for her soul and heart in every way. Even when they argued. Hell, sometimes, it was especially true when they argued.

Cady chuckled out loud to herself with the thought.

"What's so funny?" Sid frowned suspiciously, as if he already suspected that her thoughts had somehow concerned him.

"Nothing," she denied, still grinning.

"*Come on*," he prodded with an impatient, almost incredulous tone. "That smile of yours plainly shows me that you are full of falsehood. Tell me what is so funny before I beat it out of you." He grumbled the idle threat, knowing full well she wouldn't believe it.

Cady stuck her tongue out at him.

Sid pursed his lips, but the twinkle in his eyes gave him away a second before he erupted into his own deep laughter. "You are a minx."

"You know you love it."

"I love *you*," he said, his laughter gentling, his proud eyes softening into limpid pools of yellow-orange light.

They never suspected the attack. Not until it was far too late. It took them both completely by surprise, in a rare moment of unguarded weakness. The woods around them were dark and still. Unnaturally still, for no birds sang, no crickets chirped, and no breeze rustled the leaves and branches of the forest growth. They should have suspected something. Anything. But for the first time in both their lives, they were caught completely unprepared.

Chapter Three

Steffy sat bolt upright in her chair. The loud cacophonous sounds of hardcore German techno filled her ears and for a moment she was disoriented enough to think she'd dozed off during a break from spinning records at the club.

And then she remembered. She didn't have to be at work again for at least another forty-eight hours. Right now she was at home, miles or more below ground, in the world of the Shikar. Her mate, Cinder, was off training a group of young Incinerators—those Shikars lucky enough to have the ability to create and manipulate fire. Alone and able to relax for the first time in a good while, she'd napped lightly while listening to music through a pair of headphones.

She had just had the most bizarre dream of her life. Who was she kidding? It had been more than a dream. So much more. It had been a vision, clear and true, and she'd be a fool not to admit it. Panic rose in her heart as she recounted the details in her mind.

In it, she had floated invisible above a grisly battlefield. As an incorporeal entity, she had been afforded a clear, unimpeded view of the violence and mayhem occurring beneath her. What she'd seen had shocked and terrified her.

Cady and Obsidian fought giant, hulking Daemons that dwarfed any Steffy had ever seen before, even in the wastelands beyond the Gates. They had been caught off guard by the brutes, taken completely by surprise, allowing the Daemons to gain the upper hand from the very start of the fight. The earth shook with every step the Daemons took, and the trees had trembled in the path of the monsters' boundless rage and wickedness.

It had been slaughter. Like none that Steffy had ever bore witness to.

Obsidian had been killed first—after amazing feats of courage and skill—slashed open across his middle, and impaled by a Daemon's talon that had been longer than one of Steffy's arms. Cady had fought valiantly, screaming her mate's name as she threw fire out of her fingertips, into the eyes of an attacking giant. But in the end, though she managed to kill her adversary, she too had died, buried and crushed under the very weight of her fallen foe.

Steffy could still hear Cady's screams echoing in her ears, mixing ominously with the passionate music that streamed forth from her headphones.

Jerking herself back to the present, she ripped the headphones from her ears. Almost tripping in her haste, she raced to the door, calling for the one person she knew might perhaps be able to interpret or understand her dream, which she felt sure was far more than a simple nightmare.

"*Grimm!*"

* * * * *

His eyes were black and filled with bright pinpoints of white light, like tiny stars. He had seen much with those eyes. Steffy felt sure he would have some insight to give her now, as she was still shaking with her fear of the dream. He knew so much, saw so very far…

"You must believe me when I say that this is more than just any ordinary dream. I've had premonitions like this before. If it hasn't happened yet, then it will happen very soon." She felt the hot burn of tears on her face.

Grimm's hair was so dark a red that it looked black in the shadows of his room. Steffy was sure she'd never seen him without his deeply hooded cowl covering most of his head, and the dark, dangerous beauty of him nearly stole her breath away, despite her undying love for Cinder.

He hadn't said one word to her since she'd entered his private sanctuary without any warning or knock upon the door. She'd known he'd be here, known too—somehow—that he'd expected her mere seconds before she'd thrown the door open and barged into the room. He was The Traveler, after all, Tryton's right-hand man, and keeper of many Shikar secrets. A warrior of several thousand years experience, he wasn't taken by surprise easily, no matter what the circumstances.

This man was dangerous. In so many ways. But he was also her friend, and Steffy prayed that he believed in the power of her dreams, which had so many times foretold things to come. No one, before the Shikars, had believed in her precognition. Not even she, herself. But now...now she knew for certain that Cady and Obsidian were in danger. Maybe even already dead. And she had to do something—anything—to help them.

"I do believe you," he told her at length. His voice was quiet, but melodic in a way that was powerful and profound.

"Can we do anything to stop this from happening," she pleaded, "anything at all?"

His black eyes seemed to be focused on something far, far away. Outside the confines of this room, or even of this world. "You are absolutely certain this was more than just a dream? You must be sure...we must all be sure..."

"*Yes*," she breathed a deep sigh of immense relief. She'd known this man would be the one to go to with this crisis. "I'm positive. I could smell the blood," she shuddered, "and I could hear their screams. I saw everything so clearly—"

Grimm struggled to gather his wits, straightening his broad shoulders in preparation for what must come next. He worried now for his dear friends, Cady and Obsidian. Steffy was a powerful psychic and it was unlikely that her vision would be false now simply because he wished it so. And he did wish it so.

Damn the Horde...he was weary of this war. "Dwell on it no more, Steffy. It will do you no good to worry." He felt like a hypocrite saying it. "Gather the others and wait for my return here. It will take me some time to find them—Obsidian and Cady are both good Hunters, and therefore harder for me to track than most."

Steffy nodded, shoulders slumping as she hoped against hope that she'd been quick enough informing The Traveler.

Grimm rose to tower over her and placed a light hand upon her shoulder. His gaze made Steffy feel dizzy, but at the same time it was comforting in its intensity. She'd gotten his full attention—it was what she'd hoped for, what she'd wanted. If anyone could find and save Cady and Sid, he was the one to do it.

"I *will* find them," he promised her, as if he'd read her very thoughts. "I will find them, this I can promise you. But..." His eyes drifted off again, focusing on that far away place Steffy could not see. "I only hope I will find them before it is too late. We must all be prepared for the worst this time..."

Without another word, The Traveler disappeared. Steffy turned and ran to find her husband...praying under her breath to all the gods she'd ever heard of that Grimm would find their friends in time.

Chapter Four

Cady felt the force of the blow as if it were but an echo in her body and brain.

One moment she was standing at perfect ease, staring into the loving eyes of her husband. The next, she was flying through the air with a starburst of pain in her mind.

The pain was a shock, but her alarm at being caught in such an unguarded position was even more surprising, as she flew through the air and slammed into a tree with enough force to jar it from base to tip. Dimly, as though from miles away, she heard the splintering of the tree's mighty trunk as she hit, and it was this sound, rather than any pain, that let her know she'd been well and truly injured.

But she was a Shikar now, no longer human, and as such she healed quickly—if she but gathered her strength of will to do so. And she had a formidable will, no matter how badly injured.

She rose unsteadily to her feet and darted a look around the clearing, addled but not utterly impaired by her weakness. At first she saw nothing but a blurry haze of trees and shadows. But then, with a cold, terrified heart, she released that not all the tree trunks were as they seemed. Regarding one oddly textured trunk, she looked up, and up, and up its great height. She swallowed a shriek, craning her neck to see the largest, most horrific creature she could have ever imagined, even in her darkest nightmares, towering over her menacingly.

"Cady, *run!*" Sid shouted, but his voice was strained.

Cady had never run from a fight in her life, and neither had Obsidian. That he told her to flee now meant that circumstances were dire indeed.

Dire or not, she wasn't about to meet her end with her back turned from her foe. No matter how big he was.

Her anger was like a furnace. Her blood was hot as molten lava. She felt the wash of her power like the roar of an ocean wave that rose higher and higher until it utterly consumed her. That power burned hot from her scalp to her toes, and at her fingertips the power found release. Cady shot forth a blinding stream of fire from her hands, dousing the giant's legs in liquid flames that lit up the dark night.

The giant shrieked, its howl of pain so full of evil and madness that it made the very earth tremble in its wake.

Without a second thought for her own safety, Cady ran swiftly in the direction of Sid's cry. When she reached him, what she saw stunned her. At the feet of yet another giant Daemon lay her husband, bleeding upon the ground. His stomach had been deeply lacerated by the monster, who was already raising its enormous, taloned hand to administer another strike.

"*Nooo!*" Cady screamed mindlessly, racing to reach her mate before the blow fell.

Obsidian's eyes met hers, full of the fire and power of his indomitable spirit. Even in such a hopeless situation, he was a formidable warrior to the end. "I told you to run, woman," he rasped, reaching for her. But it was too late.

The Daemon struck.

Cady screamed again, tripped, and fell flat on her face. She roared her anger and growing panic, struggling to rise. Her nose was broken, blood was pouring down her face, but she neither felt the pain of it nor cared. She regained her feet again at last and raced the last few sprinting steps that separated her from her husband and the Daemon who dared attack him.

With an audible *snick*, her Foil blades burst forth from her knuckles, and she used them to launch herself at the Daemon's back and climb her way up it. Sinking the blades deep, viciously twisting them as she shimmied her way up, she felt a mad grin twisting her bloodied lips. "*Hijo de puta*! How do you like that shit, huh?"

The beast roared, kicking the body of her husband as it flailed to reach behind its back and grab her. Cady's heart nearly stopped as Sid flew across several feet of ground, his form limp and lifeless. Her rage increased a hundred fold and with it, her adrenaline.

"You fucking bastard, you monster, you goddamned Daemon!" she roared, stabbing her Foils deep into its black, slimily-scaled hide. Over and over she stabbed it, her attack so fast and so uncontrolled that even the Daemon seemed shocked by it. "Die, die, *die*, *pendejo*! Die!"

The monster was twenty feet tall if it was an inch and packed full of strength and vicious power. It tried to shake her off its back, like a dog would shake itself free of water, but Cady held on, fueled by her rage and her terror. Her Foils were both sharp *and* poisonous, but the Daemon was so large and so strong that it appeared completely unaffected by the venom of her blades. Cady valiantly made her way up higher on the beast's shoulders and, raising her arm back for a deadly swipe, she brought her blades down with the intent to stab them into the thick neck of her foe.

Perhaps the blow would have killed it, perhaps not. She would never know. For her blow never connected. She had forgotten about the other monster. And now it made its presence known to her, sending her flying through the air with but a swipe of its hand.

Cady flew through the trees once again, traveling many yards away from the clearing now, coming to a jarring rest at the base of a great, old oak. Now both of the Daemons were focused upon her, the ground shuddering with each step they took towards her. Weak, angry, and afraid—for Obsidian more than for herself, because if she died here he would be left wounded and completely unprotected—she refused to believe he was dead. She felt the bitter taste of hopeless defeat fill her mouth. In a last desperate attempt for survival, she let her power take over.

Let it consume her. Let it become all that was left of her will to fight and to triumph.

Cady freely and gladly fed the flames that seemed always to lurk beneath the surface of her skin. Knowing it was madness, knowing also that she had no choice, she allowed the fires of rage and battle to consume her. She let loose all of her control, uncaring if the resulting inferno flattened her, the forest, or even the entire town, just so long as it killed these Daemons. Just so long as it saved Obsidian, and maybe even herself, from total defeat.

The fire burned. The flames roared. Her vision blurred with the heat of it, and her blood threatened to burst from her veins like a violent eruption of lava. Cady screamed with the pain. It was too much power for her to hold, to control. She had to set it free before it killed her.

From out of the darkness, Obsidian streaked forth, Foils at the ready, to hack and slash at the legs of one of the Daemons. That he was alive and whole nearly stunned Cady into losing the last desperate hold she had on her power.

"*Obsidian*," she whispered in awe and relief, tasting the blood in her mouth like sweet, salty syrup.

Sid slashed his enemy over and over, drawing a river of black, corrupt blood from its vile flesh. The Daemon turned to swat at his attacker and tripped. It was a small stumble for a being so large and powerful, but it was enough for Sid to gain a brief upper hand. He moved with such speed and agility that Cady, eyes still blurred from the strain of holding her power in check for a few precious seconds longer, couldn't clearly see him. Unfortunately, this kept her from paying proper attention to the second Daemon, who advanced upon her with surprising stealth considering how large he was.

While she watched, unaware of the danger that lurked, Sid sallied forth with his razor sharp Foils and opened a gaping wound in the chest of the brute. Another swipe of the blades. And another. And another. And finally, at last, Sid had the creature's heart in his hands. The giant fell with a mighty crash. It echoed like a sonic boom through the clearing as it landed.

But not before taking one last swipe at Obsidian.

A talon, three feet in length and at least as big around as a man's fist, lodged deep into Obsidian's midriff, and then the Daemon fell still.

Sid made no sound. He merely sank to his knees, still clutching the heart of his fallen foe in his fists. As if the effort to move were took all of his remaining strength, he turned his head to lock gazes with Cady. Time stilled. Silence reigned. The light of his Shikar-yellow eyes dimmed and he fell to his side in the grass.

Cady screamed his name as her heart shattered into a thousand icy shards. The Daemon that stalked her moved to strike, but Cady saw him just in time to roll out of its reach. At last she released the fire of her rage and pain to engulf this remaining monster, who was so close now that she could have reached out and touched its tar-like flesh. The murky orange-red hue of its eyes seemed to hold some surprise as Cady's flames shot forth in liquid streams to burn them completely out of their sockets.

Screaming again as the power seemed to burst forth from her very skin, Cady felt, rather than saw, the enormous fireball that shot from her outstretched hands into the very center of the Daemon's chest. The release of so much power all at once made her very bones feel as if they had caved in upon themselves. She was an Incinerator, but not one as strong as this. Her level of abilities had never burned so hot or so fierce as they did now, when the hopelessness of the situation was at its peak.

Obsidian was dead. She could feel it in her heart. In her soul. He breathed no more. And without him…she had no will to fight anymore.

Her injuries consumed her. Both physical and spiritual, she was utterly and mortally wounded.

With one last mighty roar, the Daemon fell. Like a Titan cast into Tartarus, it crumbled towards the earth, knocking over trees and bracken while its chest and heart burned to dust within its own breast.

Cady didn't care. There was no triumph in her heart. She had no more strength or will to even move, and as the Daemon at last crumpled to lie still upon the ground, she found herself pinned beneath the crushing weight of one of the beast's limbs.

Turning her head, trapped at the angle that she was, she could not see past the destruction of the park clearing to glimpse the still form of her husband. Her body and her heart were broken. Her spirit crushed as surely as the lower half of her form beneath the Daemon's weight. As her breath rasped in her bruised chest, she wondered, almost calmly, what would come next?

The Daemons were back. And they were stronger than ever. She would surely die here, just as Sid had. Who would find them? Who would carry the news back to the Shikar Alliance of their defeat and passing? Would they know the truth — that the Daemons had managed somehow to pass unnoticed until the last moment, when they struck?

Cady was a Hunter as well as an Incinerator. She had the gift of knowing when these monsters lurked near. So, too, did Obsidian. Why hadn't they felt the warning of their enemies before feeling the first blow? So many questions, none of them with easy or ready answers. If only they'd been more careful. If only they hadn't underestimated the Daemon Horde. If only...

"Oh Sid," she whispered, tasting the bubbling blood in her mouth with every word. "My love, my heart, my life..." Her head roared. "Armand." She felt the sting of tears, but not much else anymore. Each breath hurt worse than the one that struggled into her lungs before it. "Oh baby, I did so want to see you become the man I know you'll grow to be...Armand."

If only he could hear her. If only Sid could have survived the attack, to live and help their son learn the lessons only a father could teach. To remind their son every day how much his

Mommy had loved him. To show him the ways of a warrior—courage and selflessness even in the face of danger or death. But Obsidian was no more. And if the fates were kind, she knew they'd be together again in the afterlife.

After all, what would any heaven be like, if she didn't have him there to argue with all the time?

A strange sort of peace engulfed her. Like the thick warmth of a familiar blanket, long loved and used. Would she, a woman long without peace in her life, at last feel the safety of Death himself as he came and took her in his arms? It seemed so perfect, even in its irony, and Cady felt her cracked lips smile.

"I'm coming soon, my love…"

"Not too soon, I hope," said a voice not too far from where she lay.

As if in a dream, Cady turned her head to see a tall, hooded and cloaked figure standing over the place where she felt sure her husband had fallen.

"Grimm," she whispered in sudden, unexpected relief.

The man turned to her, reached up, and lowered the deep hood that concealed his features. The man revealed to her was a stranger with clear, deep pools of golden light for eyes and the face of a fallen demigod.

"Don't you touch him, motherfucker!" she cried out brokenly.

He regarded her solemnly for a long, silent moment, before bending down to the ground where Sid lay. Cady could not see what he was doing, there was too much brush and disheveled earth between them.

"Goddamn it, I told you to leave him the fuck alone," she screamed.

The stranger rose once again, and this time he stalked towards her on feet that made no sound and left no footprints. "Do you kiss your mother with that mouth?" he asked haltingly, as if unused to speaking so many words at once. As if the phrase, or the very words themselves were unfamiliar to him.

This stranger was no stranger to her...she realized with a jolt of surprise and confusion. This was the man who had saved her but a year ago, from a horrible wounding at the hands of a Daemon.

"Who are you?" she asked, almost fearing his answer.

The shining-eyed savior reached out to lay one of his hands upon her. A soft, warm tingle suffused her form from head to toe. It was as if he reached inside of her to fill up all her hopeless emptiness and hurt with bright, golden, healing light. All the pain and injury of her physical form faded, as if it had never been. She barely felt the weight of the Daemon on her legs now, and had no discomfort as she lay upon the hard ground.

"Why are you helping me like this? Just who in the hell are you?" She gritted out, reaching out to grip his wrist in a furious hold.

"I am who I am and that is all you need know."

"Fucker, I hate riddles! What did you do to Sid?"

"Your mate is healed, as are you." He rose with a graceful movement that would have shamed even the greatest Shikar, and reached out with both his hands for the gigantic form of the Daemon that still pinned her.

"*Aaargh!*" Foils sliced through the stranger's middle as Obsidian streaked out of the darkness behind to attack.

"*Nooo!*" Cady called to warn Sid away, even as her heart and soul rejoiced in stunned disbelief that he was alive.

But she needn't have bothered with the warning. As the Foils cleared the form of the man—slicing completely through him in a blow that should have left him in two separate halves—naught but dust flew forth from the wound and he was left completely unharmed. The stranger turned, motioned oddly with his hand, and Sid fell back onto the ground again.

"Damn you—"

"He is unharmed." The man turned back to the Daemon's corpse, laid his hands upon it, and closed his burning bright eyes.

The giant turned to a fine dust that immediately scattered upon a sudden, strong gust of wind. Cady choked, eyes and throat stinging from the unexpected dust storm. She scrambled to her feet, avoiding the stranger completely, and lunged for Obsidian, who was already rising from his position on the ground.

"My love, my love," she cried over and over, raining kisses down upon his face even as the dust and her tears mingled with the blood that still covered their forms. "You're alive!"

"Get behind me," Sid pushed her back, eyeing the stranger menacingly.

"No Sid, he saved us. It's okay." She ran her hands over him from head to toe, seeking out injuries and finding none.

"Who are you?" Sid barked imperiously at the stranger, swatting Cady's hands away and pressing her behind him as best he could. "I don't recognize you, yet you look like a Shikar."

Silence. The man replied at long last, but all the while his eyes were locked with Cady's. "Love is my disguise. You'll soon see—"

"Lazarus, my son. You linger too long."

So many things were happening at once that Cady's and Obsidian's heads swam. They both turned to look at the newcomer whose voice had addressed their savior so familiarly.

A man who was so much more than a man entered the clearing, appearing from the darkness, as if made from out of the very shadows themselves. His bright blond hair shone like a star in the night and his eyes were black as the darkest pits of Hell. From his eyes shone death and damnation. While upon his face he wore the mask of Tryton.

"What is this?" Sid whispered brokenly. His confusion was as plain to hear in his voice as it was in the choking noise that issued forth from Cady's lips. "Tryton?"

The blond-haired man—who was Tryton, and yet not Tryton—ignored them both. He held his hand out to the cloaked man. The one he'd named Lazarus. The one he'd called son. "Come," he issued the command again.

Cady felt the hairs on the back of her nape rise. Fear and wonder consumed her. The man's voice was metallic and terrifying. There was no life in that voice, no emotion at all, only stillness. If Death had a voice, he would surely speak forth from this man's mouth. The cold, black depths of his eyes locked upon hers for only a brief a second, but that second stretched on into an eternity.

In those eyes she saw endless pain. Danger. Power. Power that could rival that of the very gods fabled in all of mankind's history. His gaze held the weight of a thousand misspent lifetimes. There was madness in their depths that stretched on for eons and beyond. But there was also something else, something she couldn't believe, and it scared her far more than anything she'd ever known.

It was regret. Endless, profound, and unguarded.

She clutched Sid to her frantically, as though afraid the dangerous blond man would take him from her.

Lazarus willingly approached the man, clearly without fear. Cady and Obsidian both knew they could not have walked so courageously towards the Tryton look-alike. Danger and insanity exuded from him like a cloying perfume.

The two men clasped hands and in a fine *poof* of dust, they disappeared completely. Nothing was left of them but the flyaway particles of earth that floated upon the air, falling slowly, gently to the ground.

"I think I'm going to faint," Cady gasped, wide eyed.

Boom. Boom. Boom.

"Shit. What now?" Sid growled, looking about.

Boom. Boom. Boom.

The heart of the giant Obsidian had felled. It was beating, loud and strong. The Daemon was going to rise, and soon, if they didn't burn the organ to ash right away.

"*Fuck!*" Cady exclaimed.

Both she and Sid dived for the basketball-sized heart at the same time. When her hands touched the sticky, black ooze of the throbbing organ's tissue, it burst into bright, hot flames. The two of them sank back down onto their haunches and watched as the enormous heart was consumed by fire until there was nothing left but ashes.

Then Cady burst into tears.

Chapter Five

Cady launched herself into her mate's waiting, open arms, sobbing as if she might never stop, clinging to him with desperate relief.

"Shhh, baby. Don't cry," he crooned.

"I thought I'd lost you," she choked out.

"I thought you had too, there for a while," he murmured. "What the hell happened? Who were those men?"

Cady felt almost sure that he didn't expect her to reply, but she did anyway. "That man, Lazarus, that's the second time he's saved my life."

Sid stilled. He held her back from him at arm's length so that their gazes could meet. "What can you mean by that? How do you know him?"

Cady shook her head slowly, wiping inelegantly at her wet cheeks. "I don't know him, I just...I just...I can't explain it, but when he looks at me..."

"He has saved you twice, you said."

"Yes. Back when Emily was leading us through New York...I might have died if he hadn't come. And now, he's saved us both. But why?"

"Who can he be?" Sid mused.

"And the other..." Cady's voice shook.

"He looked like Tryton. How can he look like Tryton and not be Tryton? This makes no sense to me," Obsidian frowned, shaking his head.

"We need to get back. To tell the others what's happened. And we need to send for Tryton right away."

Sid sighed deeply, wincing. "I am far too weak to Travel yet."

"What?" Cady jerked from his hold. "Are you still hurt? I thought that man fixed you like he fixed me. I feel fine—where do you hurt—"

"Shush." Sid put a gentle finger to her lips in an effort to stem the rapid flow of her words. "I am fine. It is merely that I am tired from the battle and from the healing. I will be right again in a few hours, perhaps."

"But we can't stay here, more of these motherfuckers might come back. I, for one, am ready to turn tail and run our asses out of here. I can't handle another attack like that without some reinforcements."

Sid chuckled and cupped her cheek in his hand. "You? Retreat? Where was this good sense when I told you to run earlier, hmm?"

Cady swatted his hand away roughly. "I'm not joking, Sid." Her voice broke. "I can't risk you again like that, not this soon. We have to get out of here."

"There is no possibility of my Traveling. And we cannot go back where there are people to witness the blood and gore upon our clothing."

"We have to do something," she cried.

Sid put his lips to hers. It was a soft kiss, full of sweetness and tenderness and love. He parted her lips and let his tongue stroke into the depths of her mouth. His hands rose up to cup the sides of her face, tilting it just so. He worshipped her mouth with his, filling her up with his breath and his taste and his scent.

Cady had never experienced such an earth-shattering kiss. It was the very embodiment of true, undying love. It broke through all of her defenses, and filled her up with something so strong and everlasting that she was made stronger than ever before.

Her arms went around his neck. His hands moved down her back, gripping her so tight and so close that their heartbeats touched and reverberated. Their kiss grew rougher, harder. Obsidian ate at her mouth as if he wanted to swallow her whole. And Cady was just as eager to taste of him, to feel his lips and his tongue caressing hers, to breathe his sighs and give him her own, to drown herself in him.

"I love you, you foolish, stubborn, courageous woman." He interspersed each word with a hard kiss upon her open, gasping mouth.

"Don't ever leave me, you big, arrogant jerk." She exhaled each word on a sigh. "I need you too damn much to let you go without following you."

His kisses moved down from her mouth to her chin and then on to her jaw. Her fingers threaded through his long, dark hair.

"My baby, my beautiful one, my everything," he murmured. Pressing the words into her skin with hard kisses that seemed to grow more and more desperate with each pass of his lips.

"Hold me," she gasped. "Hold me tight. I can't ever go through this again." Her words trembled. "I can't bear the thought of your death. Oh god, I love you so much. More than I would have ever thought possible before our first meeting."

"I was nothing but a shell before you came into my life." His hand fumbled with her clothing, pushing her shirt up to expose her breasts to his seeking, hungering mouth.

"I can't lose you, not ever. I love you," she repeated desperately.

"I'll never leave you. You are everything to me." He pressed a hard kiss to her breast, then sucked her nipple into his mouth.

"Oh god, Sid, that feels so good. Suck me hard, please," she cried, clutching him to her breast with a mad passion. "Take all of me, so I know you're here and this isn't just a dream."

"No dream could be so perfect." His voice was strained, his control nearly at the breaking point.

Cady's hands moved all over his broad, muscular back. She pulled his shirt over his head, tangling his hair until it was a wild halo of black shadows about them. The heat of his golden skin burned against her, his belly pressing down against hers, his hips settling into the cradle between her spread legs.

"I was so scared," she admitted in a small voice.

His head came up, his hands smoothing the find tendrils of hair away from her temples. His orange-yellow gaze burned down into hers. "Me too, baby. Me too."

"I need you so much." She pulled his mouth down to hers for another, deep kiss. Their tongues slid in a dance as old as time itself, and they both trembled with need and desire.

Sid's hands were almost bruising as he jerked her pants down to her ankles. "Kick them off," he commanded.

"You too," she said, when her hands fumbled at the fastening of his trousers.

When he settled back down upon her, they were pressed naked skin to naked skin. Cady's hand moved to cup and hold the heavy, thick length of his cock. He was so hard and so hot, it was like holding a live coal in her hand.

Obsidian's fingers stroked over the seam of her pussy, finding a burning wetness there that spoke volumes of her need for him. He pressed one long finger into her channel, thrusting gently in and out of her welcoming body until her keening cries filled his ears. She was so soft and so delicate, he feared hurting her with the force of his own passion.

He wanted to consume her. But he wanted to savor her, too.

Cady pumped him once, twice, then over and over until he trembled. His shudders wracked both their frames. A bead of his sweat trickled from his brow and fell onto her parted lips. She darted her tongue out to capture the salty taste of him.

Sid pulled himself free of her pumping hands. He spread her legs wide with his palms and rubbed his cock against her pussy with slow, languid movements. Her moisture bathed them both. Their sweat commingled. Their bodies ached to join, but still he held back.

With a cry, Cady took matters into her own hands. She rolled them, until Sid was caught beneath her weight. With a sensual undulation of her hips, she took him inside of her, sinking down onto his erection, like a sword sliding into its sheath after a long, drawn-out battle.

"I love you," they whispered in unison. The sound of their words echoed and trailed upon the air like a tiny wind.

Their gazes met and held. Cady rocked back and forth upon him. Soft, slow, gentle movements that drowned them both in exquisite pleasure and anticipation. Her hands were anchored, palms flat, upon the bulging ridge of the muscles upon his chest. Obsidian's hands rubbed and cupped her bottom as she rose and fell upon him.

The shuddering sound of their breathing and the soft, liquid sound of their bodies joining over and over were the only breaks in the silence of the clearing for many long moments. Cady rolled her hips in a circular movement, making Obsidian groan in bliss. Obsidian tilted his pelvis to rub against her swollen clit and she moaned brokenly with rapture.

Abruptly lifting her off of him, Sid brought her up and over to straddle his face. His mouth fastened upon her pussy, suckling her, licking her, kissing every inch of her swollen, tender flesh. Cady's eyes rolled up into the back of her head and she cried out, uncaring of who or what might chance to hear her. Nothing mattered but his hot, wet mouth rooting at the core of her.

But then it was gone. She moaned from the loss of his most intimate kiss. Sid lifted her again, standing with her. He pulled her up into his arms, holding her easily with one hand, while guiding her legs around his waist with the other. Cady sank down onto his big, thick cock again, with a sigh of sweet ecstasy. Sid's hands cupped her ass, and his hips pumped into her, bouncing her upon him.

Cady felt impaled. The soft bump and slap of his balls against her anus made her whole body quake. As if Sid knew exactly what she wanted, one of his fingers massaged firm, tiny circles into the moue of her asshole. Her nails dug into his shoulders, and suddenly their thrusts became more frantic — rougher and wilder.

They raced towards the finish together. Cady squeezed the muscles of her cunt around him. Obsidian swelled full and wide within her body, thrusting harder and harder into the heart of her welcoming body. With a shout, he pounded into her and stilled.

Cady felt her body shudder as stars appeared before her eyes, stunning her vision. Her heart thundered. Her body flushed from head to toe, and she screamed with the onslaught of her climax.

Obsidian's thick, hot cream washed into her. Her body pulsed and clenched, grabbing at each drop of his come. Sid fell to his knees, groaning over and over again in a hoarse voice as he spurted himself into the depths of her.

They clutched tightly to each other for so long, their arms and legs went numb. Their shudders stilled, their breathing slowed, and their thundering heartbeats quieted. The cool night air intruded once again, but did nothing to dispel the moment. They were both covered in dirt and muck and sweat, but it was the cleansing of their souls that made this loving so profound. This was a rebirth. A celebration of life, and triumph over death itself.

An hour could have passed. They had no way of knowing. Neither of them wanted to move from their embrace, neither of them wanted such peace and bliss to end.

But it did. It had to, for such things are too profound, too meaningful to last forever.

"Are you unharmed?"

Cady and Sid both turned to see The Traveler standing still at their side.

"We are now," Cady whispered, uncaring of her nudity, for Grimm had seen her nude more times than she could count. Indeed, he often watched her and Obsidian make love, with their willing and happy acceptance.

"What happened here?" Grimm asked quietly.

"We will explain everything. Just take us home for now, Traveler."

"Yes." Cady breathed a sigh of relief. "*Please* take us home."

Without further preliminaries, Grimm reached out with his beautifully long-fingered hands, touched both their dark heads, and took them home.

Epilogue

"What do you think they could have been? A secret group of Shikar? It seems impossible, but after tonight, I could believe just about anything." Obsidian rubbed at his temples wearily.

Cady snuggled up at his side, unable, even after the several hours that had passed since their battle with the Daemons, to let him out of her sight.

Edge and Emily, Cinder and Steffy, they were all here. Tryton's own personal team of warriors. But where was their leader? Only Grimm knew the answer to that, and he wasn't telling. They needed Tryton now, more than ever...Cady only hoped he came back, and soon.

After telling their story twice—once from Obsidian's point of view and then from Cady's—Grimm had said little. His face was as unreadable as ever, proud and arrogant as any Shikar's, but shadowy and full of long-held secrets. He was perhaps the oldest Shikar in existence except for Tryton...and no one knew for certain how old either of them were. Thousands of years old at least. It was frightening to realize that someone of Grimm's long years held such concern over the appearance of two strange men at the scene of a battle with the Daemons.

"That—that man looked so much like Tryton. Whatever that *thing* was, it wasn't a man, human or Shikar. That thing was something else entirely, even if it did wear Tryton's face," Cady said through nervously clenched teeth.

"No. He was a man, of that you can be certain," Grimm said pensively. His gaze swept the room, resting on each of them in turn. He fell silent for a long time, his black eyes—so much like those of the strange man on the battlefield—vague and far away.

"You will speak of this to no one," he said at last.

Steffy jerked in her seat. "What? But why not? The warriors need to be told about this —"

Grimm silenced her with a hard glance. "You can tell them all you want of the battle and this new breed of overly large Daemon. But you will —" he looked a them each in turn to bring home his point, "none of you, will speak of the two men Cady and Obsidian saw. This news must not travel beyond the walls of this room. Not until Tryton returns, at any rate," he added.

Edge snarled, one glowing Foil shooting from his pointed, accusing finger like a blue talon. "To keep such news from the Council is tantamount to treason."

"Fuck the Council," Grimm barked, taking them all aback. No one made a further sound, so shocked were they. "This goes far beyond their reach," he gritted from behind clenched teeth.

"Far beyond their reach? How can you say that, Traveler? The Council knows all —" Edge rallied.

"The Council knows nothing of this, pup." Grimm's voice was like a blade, cutting them all to the quick. "And they will know nothing of it after tonight. Tryton will handle this when he returns, and he will handle the Council as well."

"Will you go for Tryton then?" Emily asked, her voice a calm anchor in the storm of emotion flooding the room. Her eyes were as black and filled with starlight as Grimm's, though she had been a human but a year before.

"I will do what I must," Grimm responded enigmatically.

"Why all the secrecy? Why all the intrigue? And why do I always have this niggling feeling that you know a hell of a lot more than you're telling us, reaper man?" Cady spat angrily.

"This meeting is over." Grimm rose and made for the door.

"Who was that man?" Cady barked, unwilling to let the matter drop.

Grimm's gaze was fierce and angry when he swerved his head back to look at her. "Be thankful you do not know the answer to that. Be thankful your world is still unchanged. Be grateful each and every moment you have left that he passed you by." He stalked up to her, anger punctuating his every step. Obsidian rose to intercede, as if afraid that Grimm might lay a hand upon her. Grimm merely waved his hand and Obsidian fell with a thud back onto the couch. Silence reigned again for a tense, endless moment.

The starlight in Grimm's eyes made Cady dizzy, but she refused to look away and met him stare for stare.

And then, unexpectedly, Grimm eased back. His mouth softened and his exceedingly large shoulders relaxed somewhat.

"I have always admired you, Cady. You have a keen mind and a strong will. But let this be. For now, I beg of you, let this mystery go unexplored. Tryton will come and then we will decide the fate of all." Grimm turned Obsidian, whose anger smoldered under a scowl. "I am sorry, my friend, for striking out against you."

"I accept your apology," Obsidian gritted out.

Grimm addressed the room at large one last time. "Please. You are all my friends and I yours. Can you not trust to my words and keep faith with me? All I ask of you is silence. All will be explained when the proper time comes. I promise you."

"I trust you, Grimm. I don't like this business, but I do trust you," Emily offered.

"And I," Cinder echoed. Though his anger and worry were apparent as a halo of fire glowed about his bright blond head.

The others eventually agreed, and Grimm eased further, knowing they would keep the secret he so desperately wanted them to keep.

"The meeting is over," Grimm repeated and made for the door, leaving the group to their thoughts in his wake.

"The meeting may be over, but the war — the *real* war — has just begun," Steffy predicted with a worried frown.

"I fear you're right," Cady sighed. She wrapped her arms around the waist of her husband and felt his slide around her shoulders to hold her close in return. "May fate and all the gods of the world help every one of us, but I think you're right."

Coming Soon!

LORD OF THE DEEP: HORDE WARS BOOK IV
(Tryton's Story)

VOYEURS: OVEREXPOSED in
ELLORA'S CAVEMEN: TALES FROM THE TEMPLE IV
(Agate's Story)

About the author:

Sherri L. King lives in the American Deep South with her husband, artist and illustrator Darrell King. Critically acclaimed author of The Horde Wars and Moon Lust series, her primary interests lie in the world of action packed paranormals, though she's been known to dabble in several other genres as time permits.

Sherri welcomes mail from readers. You can write to her c/o Ellora's Cave Publishing at 1337 Commerce Drive, Suite 13, Stow OH 44224.

Also by Sherri L. King:

Bachelorette

Fetish*

Chronicles of the Aware

Rayven's Awakening

Moon Lust

Moon Lust♦

Bitten*

Mating Season

Feral Heat

The Horde Wars

Ravenous*

Wanton Fire

Razor's Edge

Anthologies

Midnight Desires

* book in print

♦ print book Primal Heat

KNIGHT STALKER
THE BLOOD TIES SERIES

Lora Leigh

Dedication:

To my Husband, RC (Tony) Leigh.

Thanks for the "bite".

Chapter One
Summer 2007

Bliss St. Claire stopped at the doorway to the private meeting room, her eyes widening considerably as she was held silent and still by the sight that met her gaze. She ignored the flaring regret, the green, blistering jealousy, and watched in awed amazement instead as her brother's friend, Cadan Gaelan, lowered his pants and released the monster of his cock.

She was salivating. It was thick and long—so thick he couldn't circle it, even with his big hand. The head was round and flared, tinted purple and drooling a copious amount of pre-cum as he aimed it at the inviting pussy spread out in front of him.

Bliss spared a hateful glance for Marissa Delareaux before her gaze went back to the stalk of male flesh disappearing between the woman's thighs. Marissa was nearly screaming as he began to work his cock inside her, but it was Cadan's expression, or rather the features of his face that held Bliss's horrified fascination.

"Oh God. Fuck me with that big dick. Fuck me, Cadan." Marissa was moaning like a damned bitch in heat, her eyes closed, her head rolling on the table, stupidly unaware of what was going on right in front of her.

But Bliss was aware. She told herself to run. She could hear the order screaming through her mind, but her legs refused to move. She watched in horrified fascination as Cadan's lips drew back, his cheekbones becoming more prominent as he lifted Marissa closer, holding her against his chest as he stood before the pool table, his cock moving slow and deep inside her cunt.

His head lowered, his tongue stroking Marissa's neck slowly, wetly, as she shuddered against him, her hips churning, moving her pussy on Cadan's huge cock as she grimaced, and slowly, horrifyingly, his canines lengthened, sharpened. The moment they pierced the tender skin of Marissa's neck, Bliss gasped in shock and fear.

Cadan's gaze met hers as his head jerked up. A small drop of blood fell from the pearly white dagger of his tooth to the sensual fullness of his lower lip where his tongue licked it casually away, his brooding gaze holding hers as he then licked the trail of blood that oozed slowly from Marissa's flesh.

Still watching Bliss, his lips covered the pinpricks, drawing on Marissa's neck as he held her close and began to fuck her harder, deeper, the tight clasp of Marissa's pussy sucking him in with a hollow, wet sound that seemed amplified in the small room.

Bliss shook her head, trying to run, terror beginning to build inside her at a rapid rate. She couldn't run. She couldn't make her legs move. She couldn't escape the horribly erotic sight of the dark creature sucking the blood from Marissa's neck as her pussy sucked his cock deep inside her.

Bliss fought to make sense of her paralysis as time seemed to stand still. Her gaze locked with Cadan's, her heart beating out of control as she told herself to run. She had to run, to hide. He had seen her; he knew she had seen him, had seen the lethal sharpness of his teeth piercing Marissa's flesh.

Fear was like a stain blooming through Bliss's mind, but even more horrifying was the arousal igniting in her pussy. It spread over her, throwing her off balance, confusing her. She liked to think she was an open-minded adventurous sort of girl, but she didn't know if she was quite ready for a vampire.

She watched him suck at Marissa's neck, his eyes black, his skin flushed as he laid the other woman back on the pool table. His hips thrust hard and fast between her thighs as his cock plowed inside her pussy. And through it all, he watched Bliss.

Watched her, his eyes flaming, stroking over Bliss's body, making her incapable of tearing herself free of his gaze.

She would never escape him. She knew it. Death wasn't a concern, but at this moment she wondered about her soul. She was so fucked. And not in a good way.

Chapter Two

Release her, Cadan ordered the creatures holding Bliss captive as he lifted his lips from the slender throat beneath them, his tongue caressing over the flesh, healing the punctures that pierced Marissa's skin.

She has seen you, the voice whispered through his mind. *She must be dealt with.*

We must be dealt with, a feminine voice ordered imperatively. *You have not finished feeding, Cadan. We're weak.*

Release her or you can fucking starve to death, Cadan snarled silently as he continued to hold the woman beneath him enraptured. His cock slid slowly, easily up her slick pussy, her orgasms and the arousal caused by the symbiots he carried within his body holding her in thrall.

You're being unreasonable, the female creature, Cerise, snapped. *You can't let her just leave. We need her.*

He paused in the strokes that screwed his cock up Marissa's cunt, testing the creatures and their resolve.

*Cadan, we can't. Not yet. Not until she's been dealt with. You know the rules...*the male counterpart, Aldon, reminded him, resignation filling the thought.

Oh yeah, he knew the rules, but so did they.

You were supposed to watch my back, he reminded them. *You failed in that. Now release her.*

He refused to allow them to take her memory of him, her memory of their meeting, the small touches they had shared until now, the need growing between them as hot as the fiercest fire.

*You're not being rational...*Cerise thought irritably.

Why was it always irrational when the female didn't get her way?

He withdrew his dick from the hot, tight clasp of the woman's body, his stomach tightening as Bliss's gaze flew to the wet length, her pupils flaring, the scent of her arousal filling his head like nothing else ever had.

Release her. Now. His hand went to the dagger strapped to his thigh, his thought clear within his head. He would not be controlled by the creatures. In all the years of his existence he had never allowed the one who plagued him to control him and he would be damned if the unwanted second would do so now.

Very well, the female snarled furiously as she lifted the psychic command from the young woman, allowing her freedom of movement once again. Bliss turned immediately, flying down the hallway as he commanded the door to close and secured the room against other prying eyes.

Quickly, his head lowered once again, his teeth piercing the slender neck as he drew more of the needed, life giving fluid into his mouth, cradling her head in his hand, listening to the beat of her heart, gauging the amount he needed versus the amount she must have to sustain her.

He lifted his head and carefully licked over the wound as she shuddered in yet another orgasm, despite the fact that his cock was no longer inside her. She moaned tiredly, exhausted now, pale from the loss of blood and slack within his arms.

Sighing in resignation, he pulled the tight skirt over her hips, lifted her slender body in his arms and carried her to the low couch on the other side of the room. Her short, dark brown hair framed a plump little face that wasn't exactly beautiful, but pretty all the same.

Straightening, he restored order to his own clothes and strode determinedly to the door. If Bliss had screamed bloody murder and told everyone what she saw, there would be no proof of it, but he didn't really care to have her face the humiliation that would ensue.

She deserves to be embarrassed for watching, the female symbiot inside him snorted rudely.

Shut her up. His thought was directed to his own symbiot, an ages-old male who had once shown a reasonable amount of common sense.

He could feel the creature's resignation and the female's disgust. Just what he needed, a damned woman speaking inside his head and causing him more trouble than he already had.

I'm not the female you need to worry about, she informed him mockingly. *The one who just ran out on you is the one you should fear. I stopped her for a reason, you stubborn male.*

He rolled his eyes as he stalked down the hall. The female symbiot always had a reason. He just didn't always agree with it.

Smart-ass, she replied snidely. *If you hadn't been so* male, *you might have felt it yourself. She's host material, baby. You just lost your chance to get rid of my obnoxious self.*

Chapter Three

Okay, so she had prayed for adventure, freedom. Something that would shake her world up and make her live, for a change. A lover unlike any other. An event, an experience that would change her life. Bliss hadn't meant learning that the man she completely lusted after was a vampire. She could have lived without that knowledge. It wasn't one of those pieces of information that she felt she needed to know.

Bliss opened her apartment door slowly the next afternoon. As normal, the shades and curtains were flung wide, the early morning sunshine piercing the room in wonderful, vibrant rays. A whimper of thankfulness escaped her lips as she rushed into the living room and locked the door behind her quickly.

She couldn't believe what she had seen the night before. She couldn't make herself shake the prayer that it had all been a nightmare. She would awaken soon. All she had to do was pinch herself enough to wake up. Because, despite what she had seen, despite the fear, the overpowering need to run, she had been aroused. Aroused and drawn to the dark vision as nothing she had ever been in her life.

It had made her so damned hot she had needed to change her panties even as she ran for her life, because she had creamed them outrageously.

She tossed her keys to the table beside her and leaned her head against the panel, breathing heavily, exhausted from her fight to stay hidden the night before, certain that she was being stalked. That the monster she had glimpsed in the bar's private room was but one step behind her...

"Well, perhaps more than one step."

Shock exploded in her chest as she turned, eyes wide, and confronted the dark vision of her worst nightmares. He stood in front of the window. The bright rays of the sun surrounded his tall, muscular body, created a halo around his thick hair and held his expression in shadow.

She blinked, certain she was making him up.

"Shouldn't you be in a coffin or something?" she gasped, her eyes wide as she felt her pussy moistening further. This was too much. She wanted to fuck a monster. She must have lost her mind.

"You watch too much television." He tsked gently, his midnight-blue eyes filled with laughter and promise. "That is the trouble with the world and those who inhabit it. They rely only on the legends and the tales passed down from generation to generation or created within the pages of a fiction novel. Yes, my dear, vampires exist." His voice lowered to a dark, sensual throb. "And the rules were never truly recorded properly."

She could hear the amusement in his voice, the cool mocking knowledge that he had won. Wet pussy or not, she wasn't going to deal with this right now. Her hands gripped the doorknob as she tried to turn it, to escape, to find a way to process this new information.

Except the door wouldn't open. Her hands twisted the knob, while jerky whimpers that should have been violent screams tore from her throat.

"Bliss, chill out." He was right behind her.

Bliss swung around, her fist clenched, aiming for his head as she swung her arm. In an instant it was caught within his broad palm as he stared down at her with dark, hot eyes.

"Such violent tendencies," he murmured, his voice rough and deep as he pinned her against the door. "If I didn't know better, Bliss, I would think you didn't like me anymore."

He was laughing at her. She stared up at him in a haze of fury, fear and arousal, seeing the amusement in his gaze as he watched her. The fury and fear she understood, but the arousal made zero sense to her way of thinking.

"I would like you better with a stake in your heart," she snapped, struggling against him as he held her easily.

"Bliss, I am not going to hurt you," he said softly as he pushed her hands against the door, his body flush against hers, trapping her against the panel as he transferred her wrists to one hand. The other stroked over her neck gently.

Bliss stilled at the touch of his calloused fingers against her skin. They were warm, rough, sending erotic impulses of pleasure washing over her body despite the fear that filled her.

"Don't you dare try to bite me," she snapped as his head began to lower.

A smile tipped his lips, the sensual fullness of his lower lip curving sexily as his gaze continued to hold hers.

"I bet you would taste delicious," he whispered, his voice taunting her as his hand cupped the curve of her neck. "Hot and sweet. I've wondered these months how you would taste, Bliss."

Bliss trembled against him, swallowing tightly as his gaze centered on her lips rather than her eyes.

"You are not allowed to bite me," she told him desperately. "I mean it, Cadan. There has to be a rule against biting me somewhere."

She tried to clear her mind of the sexual haze wrapping around her. Now was not the time to be turned on, she reminded herself furiously.

"There are many rules about biting," he murmured as his fingers caressed her neck. "I promise, it wouldn't hurt."

Bliss tried to control the rapid race of her heart, the arousal building in her pussy and the weakening tremors of fear that shuddered through her body.

He was still laughing at her. She could see it in his eyes, feel it in the air around them.

"Cadan, let me go." She struggled against him with renewed strength, certain that if she didn't break free, within moments she was going to be begging him to bite her. To fuck her.

"Will you restrain this penchant for violence and bloodshed you seem to have developed?" His head lowered, his lips smoothing over her brow. "It's not fighting I want to do with you, beautiful."

She stared up at him in surprise. His voice was thick with growing lust, his eyes becoming darker as his expression tightened with hunger. Bliss knew she was in serious trouble when she felt the juices sliding from her cunt to moisten the plump lips beyond. Her clit was swollen, throbbing, demanding that she do something to ease the hunger that pulsed through her body now.

This was the temptation Cadan was. From the moment she had first met him she had craved him. Unfortunately, seeing him for what he was hadn't eased that craving in any way.

"Look, you really don't want to bite me." She shook her head firmly as his fingers continued to stroke her neck.

"I really want to do a lot of things to you, Bliss," he told her erotically, his voice stroking over her senses like dark, rough velvet. "Things you could never imagine."

Against her lower stomach she felt his erection. Thick, hard, barely contained by the dark leather of his pants as he pressed against her. For one blinding moment, the memory of his cock, thick and hard as it had pressed into the other woman's body, overwhelmed her.

"Oh, I think I have a good idea now." She twisted against him; if she didn't get away from him, if he didn't stop touching her, she would be turning her neck to him willingly for a chance to spread her thighs for him.

Bliss had never thought herself sexually easy, but she had known for weeks now that all Caden would have to do was crook his finger and she would come running, panting and eager for the fucking she needed from him.

She couldn't explain it until she saw him with Marissa the night before. It had to be some kind of weird sexual vampire energy, she told herself. They could control people—it was what all the books said. He had to be controlling her, that was the only thing that made sense to her.

It still didn't ease the arousal blooming in her womb, though. Nor did it slow down the insidious slide of the juices from her pussy.

"Women amaze me." He sighed as he watched her. "Must you fight against me like this, Bliss? I would never harm you, surely you know that."

He watched her as though it somehow offended him that she hadn't automatically trusted in him. She wanted to roll her eyes, but for now, her fear was making her a bit more guarded.

"Uh, aren't you the vampire I watched stick his teeth into Marissa's neck?" she asked him fiercely. "God, Cadan. You fucking suck blood to survive and you want me to trust you?"

"Basically, yes." His smile was too charming, too *nice*. Nice was not Cadan. Sensual. Seductive. A charming playboy filled with wicked appeal. Yes. Nice? No.

"Basically, not in this fucking lifetime," she told him incredulously. "You can just keep your teeth the hell away from me."

He stared down at her, wry amusement filtering into the cool depths.

"Well, we might have a slight problem with that, Bliss, my love," he said softly. "Because I really, really want to bite you."

His thumb caressed over the vein at the side of her neck. His eyes flared, his cheeks darkening with a flush of hunger as she stared up at him in shock and fear.

"Don't do it." She struggled violently against him now, seeing the hunger in his eyes. "Really, Cadan. You wouldn't like it. Ask Walker, he says all the time I have ice water in my veins. I bet there's nothing good about my blood at all," she informed him imperatively as she bucked against him, fighting to find strength as each move ground his cock deeper into her lower stomach.

"I bet you taste like ambrosia," he whispered, smiling slightly as he easily restrained her movements, lifting her against him until the hard ridge of his erection pressed intimately against her pussy. "I saw you in that room, Bliss. I could see the hunger in your eyes as I fucked Marissa. Just as I've seen it for weeks. I could give you what you want."

Shock ran through her at his outrageous statement. A gasp of pure fury escaped her lips as she stilled, narrowing her eyes on him as offense swept through her body.

"You think I want your nasty cock now?" she demanded angrily. "Marissa's fucked every man in that bar. It's hard telling what kind of germs you're carrying."

He smiled slowly. "Vampires don't get sick, remember? Trust me, baby, any nasty little germs were quickly killed."

"Let me go, Cadan." The knowledge that he had fucked the bar's plaything was infuriatingly worse than the fact that he sucked blood to live. "You're dirty. I bet you didn't even take a shower before coming here."

She should still be terrified. Frightened out of her mind by the fact that he was holding her so effortlessly, his black eyes watching her with hot demand, his hard body, aroused and clearly hungry, pressing against hers. Instead, she was anger because he had fucked another woman. Not just fucked her, but bit her neck and drew the blood from her.

She shuddered at the thought as he frowned down at her darkly; his navy blue eyes, so blue they were nearly black, were less than pleased as he watched her.

"You have a very smart mouth, Bliss," he said as he released her hands slowly. "Do not try to escape. If you do, I'll pin you to the wall and leave you there for the night."

Her eyes narrowed, remembering how easily he had held her still and silent in the doorway of the bar's private room.

He sauntered away from her; the smooth bunching motion of the muscles of his buttocks beneath those black leather pants wasn't helping her libido to chill out much. If anything, it was only making her hand itch to caress the smooth muscle.

"Why did you follow me, anyway?" Her hand gripped the doorknob. All she needed was to distract him a moment.

He stopped at the doorway to the kitchen, drew a deep breath and shook his head slowly. The long, thick strands of dark brown hair caressed the cotton of his black T-shirt as the metal under her hand suddenly became incredibly hot.

"Damn you," she cursed as she jumped away from the door. "Cadan, let me out of here or I swear I'll make you pay."

He turned, leaning against the doorframe as he arched his brow questioningly. "And you intend to do this how?"

She hated male arrogance. It really infuriated her.

He smiled back at her slowly, tauntingly.

"Tell me, little Bliss, how do you intend to make me pay?" he asked her teasingly.

Teasingly? Were those deep blue eyes really filled with such complete male playfulness as he advanced on her?

"I could tell you many ways to make me pay," he suggested in amusement. "Come, baby, tease me. Let me see that pretty body and know that you are never going to let me taste you." Her breasts swelled as he said the words with low, brooding emphasis. "Touch you." He licked his lower lip as her stomach clenched in arousal. "Fuck you until we both scream from the intensity of the pleasure."

He was too close. He was towering over her, surrounding her; the unique male aura that had drawn her in the past weeks was like a cloak around her now. She ached.

"Your vampire mojo isn't going to work on me." She moved quickly, trying to pass him, only to come up short as he suddenly blocked the attempt to escape.

"Vampire mojo?" He laughed silkily, his lips curving beguilingly. "What is vampire mojo, Bliss? This is a new one for me."

She backed away from him slowly. "You know what I mean," she snapped, watching him carefully as she sought another venue of escape. "That weird thing you're doing that is supposed to make me crazy with lust."

His eyes widened as laughter gleamed in his gaze.

"Is it working?" he asked her softly. "I was unaware of this mojo you're talking about, but I would be more than willing to learn to use it more effectively. I have dedicated my life to learning such things, you know."

She sneered back at him. "You think you're so smart." She slapped at his hand as he reached to touch her. She wanted to smack his face as she heard the chuckle that vibrated in his chest.

He stalked her around the room, his big body corded and ready, the bulge at the front of his pants impossible to miss as her gaze flickered downward. She wanted to groan at the sight of it. It made her pussy cream, spasm with hunger. She could feel the silky slide of her juices along the warm folds and knew she was in deep trouble. She had never desired a man this deeply. And it was just her luck that he sucked blood for a living.

"Why are you here torturing me?" She wanted to stomp her feet at him, wanted to smack the smirk from his face as his lips tilted in that sexy curve.

"How am I torturing you?" he asked her softly, spreading his hands wide as he watched her carefully. "I am just visiting, Bliss. Perhaps I want to get to know you better."

Were there insane vampires? Evidently there were, because this one wasn't sane in the least.

"You are just not right." She watched him sadly as she shook her head.

His smile was filled with male confidence and superiority. "I've heard that said many times." He nodded, watching her carefully. "I feel I should warn you, Bliss, if you sprint for that bedroom as you are so obviously intending, then I will chase you. I will catch you. And when I do, I will fuck you."

She stopped. Her gaze went to the bedroom door once again. So near and yet so far. She looked back at Cadan.

"You are not sucking my blood," she told him fiercely. "I need it, too, and it's mine."

He crossed his arms over his chest and arched a brow curiously. "How about just a little bitty taste?" he asked her as he tilted his head to the side and regarded her with those laughing eyes. "I promise you, you will enjoy it very much."

Her heart lurched. "Just what I need," she snorted. "Death made pleasurable. Why in the hell are you here, anyway? Why did you have to follow me? And how in the hell can you stand in full sunlight? You're a fucking vampire. Don't you know better than that?"

His teeth flashed in a full smile. "Perhaps I am not a vampire." He shrugged, his eyes widening innocently. "Are you certain you saw what you thought you did, Bliss? Perhaps it was the stress of watching me fuck another," he said with false regret. "I can understand you're upset, sweetheart, really. I would have been most displeased had I caught another man's cock up your sweet little pussy. I may have even had to resort to murder had I seen such a thing."

Bliss gaped at him. Surely he wasn't serious?

"This is so insane," she muttered, glancing from the door that led from the apartment to the bedroom doorway once again. There had to be escape somewhere.

"Are you hungry yet?" he asked her, completely changing the subject as though it meant nothing at all. "I was checking out your fridge earlier. I liked the look of those steaks..."

He turned from her, heading to the kitchen, and Bliss knew she would find no better opportunity. She sprinted for the bedroom and the French doors that would lead to freedom. If not freedom, then at least someone to hear her screams.

Chapter Four

Cadan could barely contain his shout of triumph as he felt her run. He turned, watching her flee through the doorway, and sprinted after her. He was faster. He was stronger. Besides that, his symbiot was damned powerful.

Stop her, he ordered the male creature that resided calmly inside him.

Immediately he felt the surge of power that began to flow through the apartment, sealing it off, blocking her from the doors through which she had tried so desperately to escape.

"You son of a bitch!" she screamed as his arm wrapped around her waist and he threw her to the bed.

She bounced against the mattress, gasping for breath as he shackled her wrists to the bed, rising above her, his legs straddling her thighs as he laughed down at her triumphantly.

Her creamy skin was flushed a delicious pink, her sea green eyes filled with fury as she cursed him, struggling weakly to escape. Her delicate hands were clenched into fists as he released her wrists. Immediately they slammed into his chest ineffectually, more amusing than harmful, but she wouldn't be pleased to know that. Above all things, he did want to please her at the moment.

He winced in false pain as one little fist struck his chin.

"Now, Bliss, you're going to hurt yourself." He frowned as he caught her wrists once again, pretending to struggle to hold her still.

"I'm going to hurt you," she raged, slapping at his head as he let go of her.

The leather strip holding his hair back broke free then, causing a flare of frustration to spark inside his loins.

"Stay still," he growled, as he leaned over her, his long hair sliding over his shoulders to curtain her surprised face. "Look what you have done, Bliss," he whispered. "You're going to make me get all rough and bad with you. Is that what you were after, baby?"

He knew many ways to get to Bliss St. Claire. She was a sensualist, a wild woman parading as a good girl. But he had seen her fantasies, had felt them, watched them as they played out within her imagination each time he was near. Cadan had little compunction against using the powers the symbiot gave him. He never killed while feeding, he didn't cheat, he didn't steal. But he did so enjoy many of the other little side benefits. Although, to be honest, he had rarely used the ability to peek inside a female's fantasies as he had with Bliss's. There was just something about her eyes. Something untamed, something that had always called to him, made him hard and reckless.

He watched her eyes widen at his question, felt her body tremble in response.

"This is a nightmare," she suddenly moaned. "I'm trapped in a nightmare and no one will wake me up."

He had to laugh at her exaggeration. She was amazingly cute, feisty, and handling what she had seen much better than he had expected her to. She should have been screaming, crying, completely hysterical. Instead, she was angry and aroused.

Some females do know how to conduct themselves, unlike certain males I am becoming acquainted with, the female symbiot injected sarcastically.

Shut her up, Cadan ordered the male counterpart. *So help me, if she bothers me right now I'll leave her in there to torment you forever. Do you understand me?*

There was silence, blessed silence within his head then.

"Now, where was I?" he whispered as he leaned over her slowly, smiling wickedly as her eyes widened. "Ah yes, I was seriously considering kissing you, Bliss St. Claire. What do you think of that?"

Her eyes narrowed again. She looked so damned cute when she did that.

"Did you wash your dick before you came here, at least?" she snapped.

"Of course I did," he murmured as his head lowered, his lips stroking over the soft shell of her ear. "Don't worry, baby, I would never fuck you with the leavings of another woman on me. Even I am not so inconsiderate as that."

She growled furiously. He loved that little sound. The vibration in the back of her throat made his cock harden, made him wonder what she would sound like as she became more heated, as she began to lose herself in the pleasure that would grow between them.

At that moment, though, he regretted the episode with Marissa more than he regretted anything within recent memory. Had he any clue what tonight's outcome would be, he would have never touched the other woman. But it had been fuck Marissa, or rape Bliss. That was not a crime he wanted to carry on his conscience, but his lust for her was becoming nearly as overwhelming as the physical hungers the symbiots caused within his body. Driving, desperate, a need rather than a mere desire.

"I'm going to regret this, aren't I?" she finally asked him with a small groan. "I know I am. I can feel it."

"Hmm, are you certain that is what you feel, or is it this?" He moved quickly, spreading her thighs as he pressed against her. "This hunger, Bliss. I would have spared you from it if I could have. But it will not go away, nor can another assuage it, as I learned last night. I don't want to fight it any longer. I won't fight it any longer. Today, Bliss St. Claire, I will make you mine."

As he said the words, he knew the truth of them. For three centuries he had roamed the earth, fighting against the demonic Knights, doing all he could to preserve the honor and the life forms that he had found so long ago. Through it all, he had searched and never realized what he had searched for. Now he knew. He had searched for this.

She was watching him curiously, instead of with the fear he had first expected.

"You're going to bite me, aren't you?" She sighed. "Really, Cadan, I don't like being bitten. I need to keep all my blood. And that's just gross. Do you have any idea how gross sucking blood is? It's just going to make me sick, I swear it will."

He wanted to laugh in sheer pleasure. She was unlike any woman he had ever known. How could he have known that his mission to this small town would bring him such an amazing woman?

But he had no illusions that this would be easy. When she learned what he was about to do, she would be furious. She might well kill him the moment she realized.

You are certain she is strong enough for this? He asked the female symbiot. *She will not be pleased.*

She is the one I have searched for all these ages, Cadan, Cerise assured him, her thought ringing with her conviction. *She's strong, and she will accept. I'm not wrong, I swear this.*

He lowered his head, resting it against Bliss's forehead as he stared down at her. He would take her. There would be no chance of losing her should the Knights find her. They would destroy her, turn her into a pale copy of the woman she truly was, and he couldn't allow that.

"Are you going to deny me?" he asked Bliss then, his body throbbing with desire.

He hadn't expected this. He had avoided her all these weeks, knowing that his response to her was too deep, too intense to ever let her go once he had her. He had no desire to fight against the incredible response. He had fought alone for many years, knowing instinctively that the women he had met, both with and without the sentient life forms that inhabited his own body, did not possess the temperament and the love of life he knew his woman would require.

Bliss St. Clair was different. She had that love for life, but she also had an innocence, an energy, that enchanted him.

"I should." She sighed. "I really should. Because I just know you're going to do something really weird to me. I mean it, Cadan, I don't want you doing any weird shit."

"And what would you classify as weird shit, Bliss?" he asked her suggestively, smiling down at her, knowing her fears, yet seeing the adventurous streak that shimmered in her gaze.

"I don't want to have to suck blood, Cadan. If fucking you requires sucking your blood, then I don't think it's going to be worth it."

"Hmm, what would you consider sucking then?" he asked her, pressing his lips to her forehead before trailing them to her cheek, her jaw.

Her breathing began to quicken, the smell of her arousal grew thicker. She was getting hot for him, the touch of his body doing the same to her that the touch of hers was doing to him. Making him go up in flames.

He was burning for her. His cock was already fully erect, the blood pumping hard and heavy through the thick flesh. He shouldn't have been so hard, so aroused after taking Marissa the night before, but he admitted that since meeting Bliss, no other woman had satisfied the strong sex drive that filled him.

"Oh, I could be convinced to do many things, Cadan," she told him suggestively. "But I draw the line at sucking blood."

"Perhaps, then, you would allow me a small taste of yours?" he whispered as his lips moved to her neck, his tongue caressing the throbbing vein there.

He felt her still beneath him. He licked at her neck once again before allowing his teeth to scrape over the tender flesh there. His body tightened; he could feel the hunger of the creatures growing inside him, both sexual and otherwise.

Finally, Bliss shivered and moaned roughly as his hands skimmed down her side, drawing her thighs apart as he settled more firmly against her. He pressed his hips tighter into the cradle he found there, grinding the length of his cock against the tender pad of her pussy.

She lifted to him, hot and sweet, a low moan sounding from her throat.

"This neck biting thing is really weird, Cadan," she moaned as his fingers moved to the buttons of her blouse, flicking them open as his head raised to watch the incredible green of her eyes darken with her lust.

"It is more erotic than you could ever know," he told her. "It will bring you to a peak you could never experience otherwise, Bliss. I can give you paradise, if you will but allow me to."

She watched him as he flipped open the last button of her shirt and pushed the edges slowly aside.

She wore no bra. Cadan swallowed tightly as he tried to hold onto his control. Her breasts were exquisite. High and round, with perfect delicate pink nipples that hardened as he watched them.

"And I see something besides your pretty neck that I long to suckle, Bliss," he told her roughly. "Your sweet pretty nipples beckon to my mouth."

She moaned with a low, soft sound of female hunger. He loved that sound from her throat. Loved what it did to his own excitement as he heard it.

"You're dangerous," she told him roughly as her head twisted against the bed. "You're using that funky vampire voodoo, Cadan. I know you are."

He smiled down at her. "No funky voodoo, sweetheart, I promise you this. Only you and me, Bliss, and the heat growing between us. Nothing more."

Chapter Five

Bliss opened her eyes, staring at Cadan in dazed fascination as his head lifted and his gaze met hers. She had wanted adventure. She had wanted Cadan and the passion and excitement he made her feel each time she was in his presence. She should be, by all counts, terrified of him. Instead, his amusement, his playful passion and the integrity she had glimpsed in him when she met him pulled at her.

She shouldn't trust him, yet she did. She shouldn't need him, but the hunger growing in her for this man was becoming more imperative than the air she breathed.

It was that funky vampire voodoo. It had to be.

"You're thinking," he whispered, the bad boy smile that drew her so strongly tilting his lips.

In retaliation, his hand cupped her breast, his thumb raking over her nipple as his tongue rimmed her lips slowly.

"You're not allowed to think right now, sweetheart," he crooned gently. "Turn that curious little mind off."

Bliss allowed her lips to curl with amusement, though her breath caught at the sensation of his tongue licking at them. He was heated, hard, his body corded with strength and tense with demand.

"If I don't keep my mind turned on, it's hard telling what you might try to sneak by me," she panted as his teeth nipped at her lips before his tongue soothed the small ache.

The sensuality of the caress had the breath halting for long seconds in her chest. She stared into his darkening eyes, seeing the glimmer of something more than the man he was, the excitement of sharing it with her, and felt as hedonistic, as free as the life she glimpsed in his eyes. It was a heady brew.

"It would be kind of hard to sneak what I have in you, sweetheart," he murmured against her lips as his fingers tightened on the taut bud of her nipple.

The sweet ache had her clenching, her body tightening beneath his as he ground his cock into her pussy once again. Her clit swelled in response as she felt the moisture flowing from her vagina.

She struggled against the invisible bonds holding her, her fingers curling in response to the sensations that flowed through her. She wanted to touch him, wanted to run her hands over his body and feel every delicious inch of him.

"Let me go, Cadan," she whispered as his head lowered again, his lips smoothing over her jaw.

"But I like you so well stretched out beneath me, restrained," he said roughly. "Your body open to me. All mine to explore as I see fit. Will you let me explore you, sweet Bliss? Let me take my fill of your body as I fill you with mine?"

The blatant question had her whimpering in arousal. She had never allowed another man to restrain her, to take her in such a way. But Cadan hadn't really given her a choice, had he?

"No biting." She arched to him with a strangled moan as his lips moved over her throat.

"Just little nips?" She felt his smile against the hard throb of her vein just before his tongue licked over it.

Warm and moist, the gentle caress had her shuddering with pleasure.

"I want to touch you," she moaned, twisting beneath him. "Let me touch you, Cadan."

"If you touch me, I'll lose all control, woman," he growled, his voice husky, playful, yet filled with a deep, heated yearning.

From that moment on, he gave her no chance to argue further. His lips moved down her throat, his long, dark hair caressing her collarbone as he covered a hard, tight nipple.

Fire exploded in her pussy as she arched to him, a ragged moan tearing from her throat as he began to suckle at her breast. His hands were never still. Calloused and warm, they ran down her sides, shaped her hips, then moved to her abdomen and quickly unsnapped her jeans.

Alternating sensations tore through her. She could feel electricity flaring across her nerve endings, the ache that centered deep inside her cunt echoing in hard pulsing need into her clit, through her womb.

Her fists clenched with the need to touch him, to hold him to her breast as his hands smoothed the jeans over her hips, down her thighs, his lips moving lower, past her breasts, down her stomach.

As he shed her pants, Bliss shed her inhibitions. She had waited for this. It didn't matter what he was. It didn't matter who he was. Nothing mattered except the exquisite pleasure streaking through her body.

Within minutes she lay beneath him, naked, restrained, her legs spread wide, open to his voracious gaze.

"Cadan," she groaned his name weakly as she arched her hips. The feel of his warm breath against her damp flesh was nearly too much to bear.

"Damn. I'm going to eat you up, sweetheart," he told her hoarsely. "Every sweet, hot drop of cream running out of your pussy is going to be mine."

Her womb flexed in near orgasm as his words washed over her senses. A second later, she nearly screamed in pleasure as his tongue swiped through the hot, slick folds of her pussy.

Intense and slightly rough, he licked at her hungrily. His tongue circled her clit, then arrowed down once again until it was flickering against the entrance to her vagina, before licking upward again. He sucked and licked at her until sweat dampened her flesh and she was writhing beneath him, desperate for more, desperate to be filled by the thick, engorged length of his cock.

"Stop torturing me." She struggled to free her hands from whatever bound them to the bed. The heated energy was impossible to break.

"You taste like paradise," he growled, sipping at the folds of her cunt, sucking at the juices seeping from her vagina.

His tongue pushed inside her heatedly. A strangled cry erupted from her throat as her muscles tightened around his tongue, desperate to hold him inside her, to find the pressure she needed to send her hurtling over the edge.

He chuckled against the sensitive mound.

"Did you think I would make it so easy for you, sweetheart?" The laughter that filled his voice had her gritting her teeth in agonized pleasure. "Not yet, baby. Soon, but not yet. It's not my tongue you're going to be coming around. It will be my cock."

For a moment, the memory of his cock, thick and long, spearing between Marissa's thighs flashed through her mind. He had to be over nine inches long, perhaps nearly ten. She shivered at the thought. She had never known a man so large.

He moved away from her then and stood by the side of the bed, watching her carefully as he shrugged away his shirt.

Cadan's chest was broad, darkly tanned, with a light arrowing of dark hair leading into the waistband of the leather pants he was quickly releasing. Bliss licked her lips slowly as he removed his boots, then began to pull off the pants.

Her heart raced in her chest, making breathing difficult as he undressed. She wanted to undress him. Wanted to peel away those pants as her lips tracked each inch of flesh she revealed.

As he kicked his pants away, her eyes widened at the sight of his powerful cock. The head was engorged, dark, the stalk thick and hard. Her pussy began to weep in need.

"I've been waiting for this, Bliss," he whispered as he moved to the bed, coming between her thighs as she stared up at him in dazed need.

She couldn't believe she was actually lying there, waiting for him. Weeks of watching him, wondering, needing him. She hadn't thought she would ever reach this point. That she would be here, restrained, her pussy slick and hot with hunger as he moved his powerful body between her spread thighs.

"God, I know this isn't going to be easy," she panted. "What are you going to do, turn me into a blood sucker before you're done with me?"

He smiled, a wicked flash of brilliant white teeth as he ran his fingers through the hot slit of her cunt.

"How about a cock sucker instead?" he asked her softly. "Could you handle that one?"

Her mouth watered.

"You're dangerous." She fought to breathe, to make sense of the overwhelming lust that flowed through her body.

She had never needed anyone or anything with the desperation that she needed Cadan now. It made no sense. But then, the attraction that had been steadily building for the past weeks had made no sense, either. As though fate, destiny, or some mad karmic blip of life had decreed that there would be no chance of her escaping whatever was to come from this mad rush to release.

"And you're beautiful," he told her. "The most beautiful woman I have ever known, Bliss. Lying there, open and willing, knowing me for what I am and wanting me anyway."

There was a small glimmer of confusion in his gaze, as though he couldn't understand how she could or would want him, knowing the truth. She hoped he wasn't expecting an answer from her, because she was damned if she could make sense of it herself.

Her gaze flickered to the heavy length of his cock, so close to her cunt, and yet too far away to do her much good.

"Are you going to use that weapon or just tease me with the sight of it?" she asked him breathlessly. "Just between you and me, Cadan, I suspect there's several inches there you're not going to be able to use."

He chuckled at that. "Were you any other woman, I would say this is true," he told her gently. "But I can make sure you take me, Bliss. I can make certain you know a pleasure you can never imagine. A pleasure you could never touch in any other way—if you're brave enough to take it."

Chapter Six

He didn't give her a chance to consider any drawbacks. Instead, Cadan rubbed the head of his cock gently against the soft, wet folds of her pussy as he watched her. His eyes were dark, filled with power and secrets and a glimmer of laughter that immediately made her feel challenged. Dared.

"Later," she groaned. "We can talk semantics later. I swear, Cadan, if you don't fuck me and do it now, I'm going to cut your black heart out of your chest the minute I'm free."

He laughed gently, a low, masculine sound that only made her hungrier.

"You had only to ask, sweetheart," he told her gently, moving closer, spreading the lips of her pussy apart slowly.

Bliss held her breath at what she knew was coming. He was huge and she knew she was built small. She hadn't been made to take a cock as big as the one getting ready to fill her now.

"Cadan." She strained closer, though the glimmer of doubt that edged her passion now could be heard in her voice. "Please don't hurt me too badly."

He stilled. Amazingly, his expression seemed to soften, to transform. There was none of the laughter that had been there minutes before, none of the playfulness. There was gentleness, warmth.

"I will ensure that you know only pleasure, Bliss," he promised her. "Only the fiercest, most heated pleasure you could ever experience."

She felt it then. A shimmer of alien heat invading her pussy. She had thought nothing could push her passion, her pleasure at his touch, higher, until she felt that unknown sensation. It tingled, stroked, soothed and relaxed muscles that were tense and bunched with need. It traveled along the tight channel, probed at hidden nerve endings and had her crying out in agonized lust.

This was like nothing she had ever known, or could have ever imagined.

A second later, it got better.

"Oh God, Cadan!" She nearly screamed his name as she felt the head of his cock begin to stretch her further.

The first, sharp burn of the entrance blazed past pleasure, past pain. She stared into his eyes, caught by the extreme emotions that glittered there, the grimace of sexual hunger that tightened his face and knew in that moment that her entire life was about to change.

"Damn. You're so tight," he groaned. "I've never taken a woman like this, Bliss..." His voice was rough, filling with a need she had never heard in another's voice. "Watch me, baby. Don't close your eyes, watch me as I fuck you, pleasure you."

She couldn't do anything else. She was only distantly aware that the restraints had loosened on her ankles. She bent her knees, her feet flat on the bed as she angled her hips to take him easier. She was shaking, sweat soaking her body as he began to work the thick length of his cock deeper inside her.

He used short, slow strokes to work her pussy open, to fill her with the thick, hungry head of his cock. As it popped fully inside her, she groaned harshly. It was so good. So blistering hot and filled with a pleasure/pain she couldn't deny.

"More," she groaned, her head thrashing on the bed as she became lost to each sensation. "More, Cadan. I need more."

She heard his harsh male cry as he began to fill her. She was pussy-stuffed. Never had such a phrase entered her mind until now. But there was no other way to describe it. He was filling her deeper, stretching her further with each stroke of his cock inside her.

Bliss moved beneath him, her hips thrusting slowly, helping him to impale her deeper, deeper. She struggled to breathe as each new inch filled her, separating muscle and tissue until every inner nerve was exposed to the caress of his cock moving inside her.

"Almost." It was clear from the tone of his voice that he was breathless as well. "We're almost there, baby. Just a little more. Please God, sweet Bliss, just a little more…"

"More…" she panted, dazed, desperate to take every inch, to feel the hard slap of his balls against her buttocks as he fucked inside her.

His hands gripped her legs, raising them, elevating her hips to allow for the extra penetration. Bliss could hear her own screams echoing in her head as he continued to fill her. It wasn't pain, it wasn't pleasure, it was rapture. It was an ecstasy unlike anything she could have ever imagined.

As Cadan pressed deep inside her, she braced her feet against his hard biceps and worked him even deeper into her convulsing cunt.

"Sweet God." His groan coincided with an abrupt relaxing at the very depths of her pussy, allowing the final inches of his cock to slide home, his balls to press hard against her ass as the hard shaft flexed and throbbed with surging excitement.

Bliss gasped at the pleasure. She could feel her orgasm pounding at her womb and wondered if she would survive the violence of it. She could feel the power of it rapidly building inside her. Even her nipples felt as though they were pulsing with the need for release. Her clit was swollen, fully revealed by the stretching of the folds of flesh around the thick male stalk penetrating her. She was impaled, on fire, consumed by the pleasure streaking through her.

"Fuck me," she moaned, moving against him.

He was filling her, consuming her. Bliss twisted beneath him, attempting to gain that final sensation that would push her past the brink and over the edge into complete ecstasy. Fire blazed from her pussy, through her clit and into her womb. Tension mounted along her nerve endings, sensitizing every portion of her flesh as she shuddered in his arms, screaming in pleasure as he thrust inside her, hard and heavy, his thick cock branding her with rapture.

She stared up at him as the pace began to increase. Cadan's pleasure, his driving lust, were clearly reflected in the midnight-blue eyes, the glow of power that seemed to fill his gaze and the tightening of his flesh over his face. His chest heaved with his breathing, his muscles tensing as he began to fuck her harder, deeper.

"Yes," he hissed hoarsely as every hard inch was sucked greedily into her yearning body. "Take me. Damn you, all of me. Fucking take me…"

He slammed into her, a series of jackhammer thrusts that stole her breath, her sanity as everything inside her exploded, disintegrated, swept her into a maelstrom of such sensation, such pleasure, that she feared there would be no surviving it.

Distantly, she heard his shattered male shout, then felt a sudden pulsing of his cock as it buried deep within her once again and his release began to surge inside the milking depths of her pussy. Lava-hot and pleasure-potent, it sent her spiraling once again into realms of sensation so exquisite she could only sink into it, allow it to explode around her, through her, until she dissolved into the sweet effervescent mists of peace.

Chapter Seven

The last tremors of release slowly shuddered through Cadan as he stared down at where his body met Bliss's. There, skin to skin, flesh to flesh, his cock was fully embedded inside the sweet haven of her pussy as he spilled the last of his seed inside her.

How long had it been since he had found a woman who could take every inch of his enflamed erection? Since he could bury himself to the hilt and know the glorious heat of a woman's vagina caressing the whole length of his cock? More years than he remembered.

I told you, she will be the perfect host, Cerise's thought drifted through his mind as he slowly pulled back, watching, entranced as his still-hard flesh slid from her cunt.

Bliss moaned beneath him, her eyes drifting open, drowsy, her expression replete.

Shut up, he thought absently to the symbiot as he reached out and touched Bliss's pale cheek gently.

She smiled back at him, her lips curving lazily.

"Is this where you suck my blood, stud?" she asked him, amusement coloring her voice.

If only he could.

He shook his head slowly. "Not yet," he whispered as his fingers trailed between her breasts, down the damp flesh of her stomach to the soft, curl-covered pad of her pussy.

"Not yet, huh?" Her legs shifted as her arms lowered from where they had once been restrained. "You wouldn't let me touch you, Cadan. I wanted to pleasure you as well."

Cadan shook his head slowly. "More pleasure than what you have already given me would have sent us both up in flames," he said ruefully as he rose from the bed, aware of the confusion in her eyes.

"You're leaving?" Bliss rose up on her elbows, staring back at him frankly.

There was no anger in her expression, only faint confusion.

He picked up his pants and pulled them on quickly. He wanted nothing more than to lay beside her, to gather her into his arms and send them both hurtling into the madness of the passion he had found within her once again.

"I have things to do." He nearly winced at the words. How callous he sounded, how cool and aloof when he felt anything but.

She watched him with a small, sad little smile.

"Of course you do," she said softly. "Necks to bite, blood to suck, women to fuck. It must be a busy life."

There was no heat in her voice, and perhaps that stung worse than true anger would have.

Aldon, your host is a fucking moron, Cerise informed his symbiot. *Do something with him, immediately.*

He knows what he's doing. As always, there was understanding in Aldon's thoughts. *He must work it out himself.*

She's a host. My host, dammit. Don't let him walk away like this.

Be still, Cerise. Cadan knows his duties. Allow him to fulfill them as he sees fit. Only he can live with them.

There was silence then. Cadan could feel the female symbiot's pain and confusion. Similar to the confusion he saw in Bliss's gaze.

"Take care, Cadan," Bliss said softly as he jerked his boots on then reached for his shirt.

He paused. Grimacing, he stared up at the ceiling for long moments, wondering at the choices that now must be made. He hadn't faced this situation in all his years as host. This choice had never confronted him; the needs of his symbiot had never been so powerful as they were now.

Perhaps because, for once, their needs were the same.

Cadan shook his head at that thought, aware of the silence within his consciousness as the alien presences watched him carefully. Just as Bliss was watching him now.

"I need the blood to survive," he told her softly. "The same as you need the air you breathe, the water you drink, I need the blood." He turned to her then, seeing the quiet concentration in her eyes as she took in each word. "I'm not dead. I don't turn into mist, nor can I take wings like a bat. I'm not a monster, though trust me, they exist, and neither am I some creature that can perform great feats of evil works. I'm a man, Bliss. One who made a choice ages ago, and until this day, gloried in the freedom it has always given me. But in this moment, I realize how tight the shackles about me truly are. I can only plead your forgiveness in involving you in such a way."

She tilted her head curiously as he finished speaking. Cadan jerked the shirt over his head as raw disgust filled him. For centuries he had fought and laughed and partied his way through the years, enjoying each second. Every battle, every wound, every triumph had been like a heady brew. But nothing had been as intoxicating as coming inside Bliss.

"We had sex." She shrugged carefully. "Now you're walking away. No recriminations, no tears or fury, Cadan. Yet, you're upset anyway. Why?"

She lay there in her nudity, her high up-thrust breasts tempting him. Her rounded stomach, the plump softness of her thighs, the sight of his seed marring the crisp dark curls between them filled him with such male satisfaction that it made him nearly euphoric.

His gaze came back to her. "I am just a man," he said again. "A host to a life form that requires the blood. One I can never live without, ever again. But since two evenings ago I have also been host to a female symbiot who lost her own in a battle with those I fight. You, Bliss, are a perfect companion for that life form. Strong, young, filled with the need for adventure, for freedom.

Make him stop! Cerise was screaming within his mind now. *Aldon, he will ruin it all. Make him stop.*

There was no answer from Aldon.

Bliss was watching Cadan in shock.

"The blood I take feeds those life forms. Without it, they will feed on mine until there is nothing left of either of us. To me, it is a more than adequate exchange. No one is harmed, and I live my life to the fullest."

"How…" She swallowed tightly. "You're saying there is something inside you?"

She was clearly struggling to understand and yet was fighting the knowledge.

"There are two somethings inside me," he told her. "And unless you want to learn what my life is about and the very nature of who and what I am firsthand, then you had better run, sweetheart. Run hard and fast because you would make the perfect mate, and I am a man desperate, not just for the woman my soul has claimed, but also for the host this damned big-mouthed symbiot inside me is raging for."

Cerise was screaming in his head. Fury pounded at him in waves, female fury, lightning-hot and filled with pain. She needed a host of her own or they would all die.

Bliss rose slowly, dragging the blanket around her as she stared back at him in disbelief.

"Vampires don't have life forms," she told him, her voice caustic. "They're infected or something. Not inhabited."

Cadan snorted with bitter amusement. "Baby, you've been reading way too many fiction novels," he drawled mockingly. "I'm not infected or damned or cursed, and the love of the perfect woman isn't going to save my black soul. Truth be told, my soul is no blacker now than it was in fourteen hundred and fifty seven when my Druid father convinced me to sacrifice myself to what he believed was a god."

He laughed over that one often. Mordan expected Cadan to emerge from the caves, depraved and filled with power. He had been more than astonished to find a stronger, undefeatable Cadan as filled with laughter and pranks as he ever had been, but also one who saw the black heart his father possessed. Ever since that day Cadan had fought to protect what Mordan would destroy. The honor and innate purity of the symbiots.

Bliss shook her head. "Fourteen fifty-seven?" she said hoarsely. "I think you're too old for me, Cadan." She inched slowly across the bed away from him.

Cadan had to restrain himself, to hold back, to keep from straddling her scrumptious little body and fucking her silly as he fed from her graceful neck. Damned symbiots. Sex and blood sucking were a powerful aphrodisiac. If it weren't so important that Bliss be at full strength to accept Cerise...

He tensed at the thought.

No, he snapped at the silent female symbiot. *I won't be worked so easily.*

There was a measure of surprise that filtered through his brain.

Don't blame me for these small glimmers of intelligence you're showing, Cadan. I was being silent as ordered, Cerise mocked him, anger echoing in her thought.

He gritted his teeth, thankful that he couldn't wring her damned neck.

"I am likely much too old for you, Bliss," he said then. "Too old, too jaded and too much of a risk."

He remembered seeing the wasted body of Cerise's host. The woman, though experienced in fighting, had been an easy mark for the Dark Knights. They had surrounded her, catching her weak from lack of blood due to her hesitancy to feed from her own people. It had killed her. It was a hesitancy he feared Bliss would share.

She rose on the other side of the bed, her black hair framing her heart-shaped face like a cloud of midnight silk, her green eyes watching him warily.

"You're agreeing too easily." She narrowed her eyes in suspicion. "Why don't I trust agreeable men?"

You are making me so mad, Cadan. She is perfect for me. If Cerise could stomp her foot in fury, she would have.

"You should trust no men." He sighed wearily.

He didn't want to leave her. He wanted to laze in that big bed the rest of the day. Nap with her, hold her, fuck her until they both collapsed from exhaustion. He wanted to laugh with her, fight with her and stay by her side—and that terrified him. He could see her watching his back, filled with fire and fury as she fought him with their enemies. He could see her broken and bloodless, staring through empty eyes, her face frozen in horror. Dead. Taken from him forever.

"Watch yourself," he muttered as he turned quickly from her. "Goodbye, Bliss."

He walked from the bedroom one step at a time, forcing himself to leave her, to walk away as he knew he should. Honor had never plagued him in the past and it bothered him that it did so now. Not that he wasn't honorable, he assured himself, it was just that the choices had never been in conflict with what he desired for himself. But now, what he wanted most could well be the death of him, because he didn't know if he could survive in a world that Bliss did not inhabit.

Chapter Eight

Oh, when I get my host I'm so going to kick your ass! The female symbiot wasn't in the least pleased, but neither was he, Cadan thought. Leaving Bliss had been incredibly hard to do.

Shut up, Cerise, before I turn you over to some ugly old toad with rotting teeth and stinking armpits, Cadan threatened her darkly. Her discontent was wearing on his nerves.

So she didn't have a host. Big fucking deal. He had to deal with a female symbiot with perpetual PMS and a bad attitude to boot and he was getting damned sick of it.

You wouldn't dare! The mental gasp was outraged.

Uh, yeah, he would. Perhaps it would be best if we allow Cadan to work this out himself. Cadan could hear Aldon's amusement at the female and he didn't appreciate it. He was being flooded with female hurt feelings, confusion and anger and he didn't like it a bit. Damn, the creature was as contrary as hell one minute and full of soft feminine hurt the next.

I can't believe you, of all symbiots, chose such a stubborn, intractable creature. It makes no sense to me at all. You've grown weak in your old age. Yep, there was the feminine hurt mixed with a sarcasm that could have cut the thickest skin.

At least I'm not a harpy with little else to do but torment the host providing me a haven in my time of need.

Cadan was stomping in anger by the time he entered his own apartment, several blocks from Bliss's. The symbiots were fighting amongst themselves now, which would have been fine indeed if they would have bothered to do it a little less strenuously within his head. They were giving him a frigging headache. Just what he needed.

He threw himself down on his bed and turned his head to look at the sunlight behind the curtains. The Knights would be moving out soon. They would creep from their shadowed places, their dark dens, and move about the city searching for the violence and pain they so enjoyed.

He closed his eyes at the thought. The Dark Knights had been created in his time by the newly arrived symbiots searching desperately for life. The last of the symbiots' energy had been used to escape their exploding spacecraft, after gaining their freedom from those who had stolen them from their home world.

The Dark Knights were a band of warriors, depraved, evil, searching for the riches and power that were rumored to be hidden within the land of Cadan's birth. Instead of riches they found the hidden power.

The Knights had burst into the cavern where the life pods had held nearly two dozen of the creatures. They had crushed the metal containers, releasing the sleeping symbiots, forms of energy and light that must have a host to survive.

Desperate to live, the symbiots had flowed into the human animals ravaging their resting place and fell victim to the madness that inhabited them. There had been no stopping them. For centuries Cadan had searched for the Knights in an attempt to release the symbiots from their prisons and to find pure hearts, worthy honorable hosts for them to inhabit instead.

Not that killing the Knights was easy. It was damned hard. They stayed bloated on terror-laced blood, strong and cunning. They were the most dangerous creatures on the face of the earth. And they were searching for the few remaining capsules that housed the symbiot warriors awaiting hosts. God help the world if they managed to find where Cadan had hidden those capsules.

If only he could find more of the lost containers that sustained the symbiots when there were no hosts. Then he could get rid of the smart-mouthed vixen arguing with his own symbiot in his head. Dammit, he needed to sleep, not to listen to the two of them trade insults.

Do you honestly believe just walking away from her is going to solve this little problem he has? Cerise questioned Aldon furiously. *You know what will happen, and yet you let him merrily walk away.*

Enough! The sudden strength of Aldon's thought had Cadan tensing in warning.

Silence filled his head now. Cadan sat up slowly, frowning.

Do we have a problem here? He asked them both carefully.

There wasn't a thought to be found from the two. For the first time in all the years he had fought with Aldon, he realized the symbiot was holding back. There was information, knowledge that Cadan hadn't been given access to.

You swore complete fealty to my life, my safety and my happiness, no matter what that might be, Cadan reminded him. *Withholding information would be a contract breaker, I believe.*

He could feel the discontent moving through him.

Cerise, would you like to find a new host on your own? He asked her silkily.

He could never rid himself of Aldon and live, but Cerise was another story.

If I could tell Bliss was host material, then the Knights can as well. Remember, their female symbiots inhabit male bodies, unable to breed or to reproduce. As long as this is true, then the world is safe from the creation of more like the Knights. But if they find her, it would be easy for Mordan to kill one of his followers and to have the girl awaiting the symbiot as it flows from its host. It would then be a simple matter to enchain her, rape her and breed her time and again.

If it would be so easy, then why has it not been done before? Cadan fought back the fury that the mention of his bastard father brought.

Because, the females have a cycle, Cadan. One century out of every six they are able to breed along with the female host. If impregnated by a male who carries One of the Light. It was a term Aldon often used to describe the symbiots, because of the pure white light of their energy forms. *Then the child that is born will carry its own immature symbiot. Kill the child, the symbiot can then be taken, placed with a dark host and the instinct and power that grows within it will be at the mercy of the host. There will be no safeguards. There will be no handicaps. It will be pure evil.*

Chapter Nine

The Knights. Cadan processed the information that Cerise gave him while a somberness he fought to keep buried moved through him. They were more than just Knights really. Several were family members, and despite the name they carried had never been knighted in any way.

The Knights were once the scourge of England, carrying the titles yet betraying the trust placed within them in ways that made Cadan cringe at the thought of the pain they had inflicted.

As he drew in a deep breath and headed back to Bliss's apartment, he realized that a time he had long feared had finally come. He had danced through the centuries, no responsibilities other than ones he had imposed on himself weighing him down. He had been careful with friendships; he didn't like losing friends. They aged and died far too quickly. Cadan retained his youth due to the symbiot's amazing powers and the immortality it afforded him. As long as he kept the being fed, he would enjoy an almost limitless life, as well as powers only dreamed of by others.

Powers that had drawn his father. He rubbed at his chin wearily, grimacing at the thought of Mordan. Another of those experiences he preferred to pretend didn't happen and yet he lived the consequences of it daily as he battled the Knights and struggled to find a way to save the symbiots they carried.

His life then hadn't been free of danger, but Cadan had embraced each day. He lived for knowledge and freedom of his father's dark life, awaiting the time that he could finally break free of the small tribe he lived within. It was on the dawn of that freedom that he had been brought to the sacred caves.

There, two dozen large pod-like casks had been discovered in the farthest cave. There, his father had convinced him to open the warmest cask, which sat in a place of prominence within the room.

Normally, he would have refused any directive his father gave. But as he touched the cask, relying on his own inner sixth sense, he had felt a peace and yet a cry for freedom that touched his soul. When he released the locks at the side, pure energy and light had swept over him, around him, then infused him with such power and strength he had collapsed against the onslaught.

Desperate, filled with hunger, the symbiot had fought itself as it tried to comfort Cadan into the transition. But the hunger had been impossible to deny. Before Cadan could give a care for the other pods he had searched first for blood. Not the evil, tainted blood of the father who watched with calculated greed, but the power of innocent life, lust, passion, laughter. He had gorged on the blood of the villagers, never killing one, but leaving them weak, weary, as he feasted.

Finally, days later he returned to the cavern. Many of the casks had been destroyed, broken open, their symbiots gone. Those that remained were damaged, the life forms inside slowly fading from existence. The race to save them had been filled with despair, yet he had done it.

Twelve of the beings had been taken by Mordan and the Dark Knights that had been the scourge of the countryside. Another dozen were left, protected within the frail pods until Cadan had been able to find them hosts worthy of their honor.

But even that had taken time, because by then Mordan and his Knights had destroyed the village. The people had been drained of their blood, men and women alike cruelly raped and abused as the evil minds that had taken the symbiots used their power for their own ends.

Cadan had spent his life fighting those Knights and searching for the remaining groups of beings that had come to Earth so long ago searching for peace. He had found hosts for those that Aldon had led. Two other groups were hidden safely now, until hosts could be found for them as well. But still, the Master was missing. A group of three pods, the most powerful of the beings, the greatest warriors ever known to walk upon land, and they had disappeared without a trace.

It was those three that Cadan searched for now, because only one of the most powerful warriors could destroy Mordan and his group. Cadan had fought for centuries, but there was no way to save the symbiots until he managed to repair more of the pods. Killing Mordan's men meant destroying those symbiots if the pods weren't ready for them. The difficulty in his task was making him insane. Being without the backup he needed, namely the other warriors he had fought with, was making it worse.

It seemed there were more groups of the symbiots than even Aldon had known of, because suddenly, the presence of vampires across the world was being whispered of. He had sent the others to investigate those rumors. Were they vampire, or were they warrior?

He didn't bother knocking when he came to Bliss's door. He mentally ordered it to open and Aldon supplied the force that did just that.

He walked into a nightmare. There was no blood, no screams, no weapons or battle. There was soft, curvy female staring at him from the couch, her legs splayed as she slowly worked the shaft of a dildo into her overexcited pussy.

It might seem like a dream come true, but the jealousy that flared inside him for the inanimate object was more than he could contain. Before he could stop himself, before Aldon could caution him in regards to his temper, he enforced the mental demand that it be gone. Out of his sight. Away from the soft, tight channel he had marked as his own.

Instantly the dildo was pulled from her pussy. The soft sucking sound of her flesh as it exited had his blood pumping furiously through his body as the adult device was flung against a far wall.

Bliss's eyes rounded with fear, then with anger as she moved to jump to her feet. She wasn't going anywhere as far as he was concerned. Before she could do more than lever herself up on her elbows he was there. His head pushed between her thighs, his lips latching onto her swollen clit as his hands gripped her hips and held her in place.

She was his woman. His pussy. He would not let her find her pleasure without him. It was unnatural. It was wrong. His cock was throbbing like an open wound beneath his pants, demanding his possession of her. His mouth watered at the taste of her, spicy and hot, more addicting than the most lust-filled blood he had ever taken.

And speaking of blood. He could hear hers. It pounded through her veins with an edge of excitement that only spurred his own higher, reinforced the claim he was making on her, and assured him that in taking her, he would be pleasuring her rather than forcing her.

Her juices were thick upon the satiny flesh of her cunt. Her clit was hard, engorged; the smell of her need was like a potent aphrodisiac that had his head spinning. She was soft, slick and so hot upon his lips and tongue that he felt his heart sear with the sensation.

"For me," he growled against the sensitive little bud. "Come for me. Only for me."

His lips suckled at her, his tongue lashed at the throbbing nubbin as she writhed in his arms, crying out her pleasure.

Yes. Her pleasure. He could feel it pumping through her body, but he needed more. So much more. He needed her screaming. He needed to know, to reinforce upon her that her pleasure came from him. Only him. He alone would bring her to climax. Not a toy or another man, or her own fingers, only him.

He moved one hand between her thighs, pressed three fingers together and nudged at the slick opening of her vagina. She bucked against him. He held tightly to his patience, struggled to prepare her easily, but the sight of her fucking herself had stolen his control. He pressed inside her forcibly, feeling the soft tissue give way, hug his fingers, ripple around them in response and grow ever wetter.

"Cadan. Oh God, I can't stand it," she cried out desperately.

Yes, this was how he wanted her. Maddened with the carnal demand streaking through her body. He wanted her as insane for the coming climax as he was to taste it. To feel it flowing from her tight pussy and filling his mouth.

He thrust inside her hard and deep, glorying in her cries and finally, blessedly, her demanding screams.

"Damn you. Fuck me. Fuck me, Cadan, now." Her hips were rising and falling quickly, following the movements of his fingers as he increased the pressure against her throbbing clit and edged her into the release she needed so desperately.

She exploded. Her cunt tightened on the plunging digits, her juices flowing eagerly as he pulled his fingers back and capped his lips over the small opening, his tongue plunging forcefully inside her as he tore at the snap and zipper of his too-tight leather pants.

She was still shuddering from the force of her release when he rose above her.

"I'm sorry," he groaned, aligning his cock with the center of her body. "I'm sorry. I can't wait."

He rose to his knees, his fingers wrapping around the width of his erection, watching as the engorged head tucked between her delicate pink pussy lips. The folds of flesh spread around the purpled head, molding to it as the thick syrup of her juices heated it further.

He was shaking with his need to push inside her, to take her hard and deep as he had earlier.

"I don't want to hurt you," he gritted out, his hands gripping her thighs and raising them as he spread her wide. He wanted, *needed* to watch as he possessed her.

"Damn you, I'm going to cut your heart out if you don't do it," she cried out passionately, filling his heart with emotions he was unaccustomed to. Tenderness, affection—no, more than affection. Deeper. Stronger. The emotions filling him were powerful, intense. And the lust was making him insane.

He could contain his own needs, he had done so for years, but he couldn't fight hers as well.

He pressed inside her. He didn't slowly work his cock in as he would have done at any other time. Instead, he forged inside, gritting his teeth at the tight heat, the rippling caress against his overly sensitive cock. Pushing into her was exquisite. It was paradise—her cries as she writhed beneath him, her demands that he fill her, take her harder. The tight, wet heat...

Cadan's head fell back, his eyes closing as the pleasure swamped him. He pumped inside her, burying his cock to the hilt, groaning at the utter complete ecstasy of having her take every hard, thick inch he had to give her.

Gripping her hips, he lifted her, going to his back on the couch as he pulled her over him, never losing possession of the hot grip around his erection as he changed the position.

He stared up at her, grinning wickedly at the passionate confusion on her flushed face. When his legs were stretched out fully, he held her hip in one hand and pressed against her stomach with the other.

"Lay back," he whispered, guiding her to lie flat along his legs as he gripped her knees. "Give me your legs."

He guided her into the position, pulling her legs over his chest as she stretched out on top of his. He snapped his teeth together at the incredible tightness and friction of her rippling pussy along his cock.

She was whimpering now, shuddering, her hips rotating as his cock began to slide more fully into the uppermost portion of her vagina. There, where the thickness of the head or the shaft didn't matter unless the position was just right to apply the correct amount of pressure against her sensitive G-spot.

Mewling, kittenish cries were coming from her now as sweat ran along his body. Holding back was killing him.

Gripping her ankles in one hard hand he reached along her body until he found the little curl-covered patch of her mound and the swollen distention of her clit.

"Now," he muttered fiercely. "Now, baby…"

He began pumping fiercely inside her as the tips of his fingers raked her clit. The extreme grip she had on his flesh kept his thrusts shallow but hard, driving into her, raking over the little bunch of nerves deep inside her convulsing flesh.

"Oh God. Cadan…" Her voice rose as the sensations began to build.

His fingers and hips moved faster. Harder.

"Cadan. Oh God. It's killing me. It's killing…"

He felt her orgasm then as he had never felt another's. The muscles of her cunt clamped down, flexed, drawing his release from the head of his dick like the eruption of a geyser. His hoarse male shout mated with her feminine scream as she began to buck in his grip, orgasming with a violence that filled him with such a rush of male pride that his chest clenched with the emotion.

They were shaking, shuddering. The hard blasts of his semen overflowed the tight confines of her clutching grip, the warmth of their mingled release flowing between them as they collapsed against the couch in exhaustion.

Stud! Cerise's thought, no matter the awe that filled it, jarred him from the euphoria that had wrapped around him.

Go away. He didn't have the strength or the energy to push her back.

Our time is nearly up, Cadan. Regret emanated from her. *We must get her agreement soon.*

Not yet. He didn't want to spoil this. This connection, this bond, as he pulled Bliss back up his body, cradling her head against his chest as she attempted to regain her composure.

His arms wrapped around her, sheltering her, holding her against the heart that had searched forever for her.

"Not bad, stud," she murmured against his chest.

For one crazy moment he wondered if Cerise had disobeyed his mental commands to wait and had flowed into Bliss without his knowledge.

There goes the glimmer of intelligence I thought I glimpsed before, Cerise mocked his thought.

"Not bad yourself." He ignored the inner voice as he pressed his lips to Bliss's forehead gently. "Not bad at all, baby."

Chapter Ten

Silence stretched around them for long moments before Bliss sighed deeply and pushed herself out of his embrace. She kept her face turned away from him, kept her fears to herself as she stood shakily, found her bearings and then walked to the chair where she had thrown her robe earlier.

"So, what made you decide to come back?" she asked carefully.

She had thought he was gone forever. A part of her had even been glad he had left. The information he had given her still hadn't really sunk in. It was hard enough to believe that vampires existed to begin with. But vampires who refused to obey the rules she had read in countless books were even worse.

She heard him moving behind her. He hadn't even removed his pants and boots before taking her. He had done no more than push them below his well-rounded rear enough to give his cock freedom before he took her.

She should have been insulted. Instead, the muscles of her stomach clenched in pleasure at the thought. This was so weird, she told herself caustically. As though there could be a future with a blood sucker.

"I came back for you," he finally answered, his voice soft. Gentle. "Did you think I wouldn't?"

"Well, you sounded pretty determined not to." She shrugged as she pushed her hair from her face, tucking a loose strand behind her ear absently. "You don't seem the type to go back once you make up your mind."

She looked over at him. He sat on the edge of his couch, his elbows resting on his knees as his arms draped between them. His shirt was gone; his hard, tanned chest was broad, a scattering of coarse, dark hair marring the smooth perfection. A tattoo graced one of his muscular upper arms. A Celtic design that wrapped around the bulging bicep. It was incredibly sexy.

"I'm not," he said, his voice low, gentle. "And there is our problem, Bliss. I've decided I want you to keep me. I can't let you go."

Shock held her rigid. She turned fully to him, staring into his somber expression in disbelief.

"Keep you? The playboy vampire?" she asked him mockingly. "What kind of game are you playing here, Cadan? Whatever it is, I'm not in the mood for it."

She pushed her hands into the pockets of her robe. Her palms itched to smooth the long strands of his hair back from his face, to caress the sharp angles of his cheekbones, the fullness of his lower lip.

He was becoming an addiction. One she could ill afford.

"It's no game." He sighed roughly, watching her with a depth of emotion in his dark eyes that tugged at the feminine core of her soul. "I tried to walk away. To save you from my world, Bliss. A world I didn't want forced on you, but one you won't be able to escape now simply because of who you are."

"And what's that?" She tilted her head curiously.

He looked angry, but more at himself than at her.

"A host," he said regretfully. "Your body, mind and heart are all perfectly created to host a female symbiot, such as I currently have tormenting the hell out of my brain. This is what I wanted to save you from. From being like me. From terrifying you with the bond that's already growing between us."

Bliss stilled her shudder as he watched her so seriously.

"You know, when I asked for adventure and freedom, this wasn't what I meant, Cadan," she snapped. "A blazing affair. A trip abroad. A fucking cruise would have been nice. A vampire with a hero complex and a dick as thick as my wrist wasn't what I was asking for."

She meant to shock him, but his grin was nothing less than sin.

"You have a very delicate wrist, sweetheart," he murmured. "I actually think it's thicker than your wrist."

She wouldn't doubt that in the least.

"You aren't allowed to bite my neck," she told him fiercely. "I need my blood, I told you that already. And I'm sure as hell not into the taste of it myself. You can keep the little aggravation you have all to yourself."

He smiled wryly as he shook his head, watching her with a glimmer of amusement.

"You felt it both times we were together, Bliss," he told her. "You wanted it. You wanted my fangs buried in your neck, wanted to bite me just as fiercely as I needed you. You can't deny it."

"The hell I can't," she snapped. She had no remorse in lying when it meant life or death. "You're a mean, lean, fucking machine, Cadan. But becoming a corpse just isn't my thing."

"I really must burn your reading material," he chuckled. "You don't die, Bliss. You aren't a corpse. You can still walk in the sun, wear a cross and swim in a pool. Where these farcical rules came from I have no clue."

"You have to suck blood. That's just gross," she argued.

"You want to suck my blood." He stood to his feet, towering over her, his voice dropping, deepening with sensual undertones. "I can feel it. Your need to taste me, to know me. You want the freedom and the power, but even more, you want me." He stepped closer, holding her mesmerized with the rough, sexual quality of his voice. "Deny it, Bliss. Go ahead and lie for both of us, because we both know that need is there inside you."

She really should voice the lie, but she couldn't. She could only stare back at him, fighting herself more than him, terrified at the choices she wanted to make.

"I wanted to be a lion tamer when I was a teenager. I grew out of that, too," she finally snapped, moving away from him, watching him carefully.

"And you think you will 'grow out' of this need you have for me now?" He was clearly laughing at her. "Sweetheart, it won't happen. Take it from me. I've lived centuries and never known such powerful emotions as I do when I touch you, hear your voice, feel you touching me. I've fought it for nearly two months now, the same as you have. This isn't just going to go away. You know better than that."

"I can hope," she snarled back at him, hating the truth in his words. "Blood just isn't my meal of choice, Cadan."

"And you believe this is all that sustains me?" he asked her incredulously. "Really, Bliss, you've seen me eat."

"Have I?" she asked him fiercely. "How do I know I have? You could have been doing that voodoo thing that vampires do. How do I know what I've seen?"

Cadan growled. A sound of male frustration that almost, just almost, had her smiling. Her brothers did that around her often.

"I wish I knew vampire voodoo." He propped his hands on his hips as he watched her with brooding ire. "You wouldn't be arguing with me. You would be eagerly taking this smart-assed excuse from an alien out of my head and into yours. And why I am even suggesting it boggles the mind. You make me crazy enough on my own."

She arched her brow mockingly. "And become a blood sucker?"

Why wasn't that thought as nasty as it should be?

Cadan pushed his fingers wearily through his hair. "They are energy forms, Bliss. They survive on our blood; their incredible power is shared with us, their knowledge, their ability to heal us to keep us from aging. It's all given to us freely. They provide us with the ability to take in more blood, to replace what they lose. It's a small exchange."

"It's eternity," she whispered, thinking of her brother.

They were the last of their family. They had no one but each other.

"It's more than just immortality," he told her softly. "It's the chance to live all your dreams, all the adventures you've ever longed for. A chance to save a race of beings who are so much more than humans will ever be, Bliss. They deserve life as well."

Bliss stared back at him, confused. Aching.

His voice vibrated with his belief, with his love of life and who and what he was. He was as free as the wind, as wild as a storm. All the things she had longed for herself. And he could give her the chance to know it all.

"Give me a chance," he finally said. "We'll take it slow and easy, Bliss. You have time to decide if you can bear immortality with me. If you can live with the battles we'll have to fight. But your choices are limited; unfortunately, it will come down to accepting the banshee in my head, or the one my enemies would force on you. Because hosts are what they search desperately for, female hosts they would kill their own for. And I won't let them take you. Not as long as I live."

Silence stretched between them as Bliss tensed at this new bit of knowledge.

"You know, Cadan," she swallowed tightly, "I'm beginning to regret the fact that the books are wrong. Because honestly, right now, I could get very, very inventive with a stake. And I'm not talking the cooking kind."

She turned away from him and stomped to her bedroom.

"I need a shower. I need peace. Go away and at least let me think without the temptation of your cock making it worse. Go bite somebody or something. Just leave me the hell alone."

Chapter Eleven

Hours later, after Cadan informed her he was indeed going to go bite someone, Bliss slipped from her apartment and walked the short distance to the bar her brother owned and tended.

She couldn't believe the course of events she had managed to bumble her way into. It was just her luck. The man of her dreams and he sucked blood to live and came with enemies that she didn't need.

The thought of those enemies sent a strange shiver up her spine. Then again, the sudden silence of the night wasn't helping. Her steps faltered as she stared around the deserted street. It was never deserted.

"Well, look at the little pretty we've found, boys. And doesn't she just stink of our wayward son, Cadan?"

The group of men stepped from the shadows of the alley, blocking her access to the bar, crowding her toward the inky blackness they had come from.

Bliss stared at them, her heart in her throat, fear exploding through her chest. She had once thought she couldn't know more terror than she had the night she had seen Cadan feeding from Marissa's neck, but she had been wrong. That had been no more than shock, no more than surprise, because terror sounded like a serpent's hiss, smelled like death and stared at her with strangely red, glowing eyes.

Bliss moved back quickly before jumping to sidestep one of the three men waylaying her. A chuckle, dark and deadly, sounded an instant before one of the creatures blocked her escape, smiling back at her, his fangs long and sharp, deadly and shining in the moonlight.

"She's a pretty little breeder, Mordan," one of the others spoke up, the middle dude, the one with the red Mohawk that looked like a rooster's comb in the center of his head. If blood didn't stain his chin, lips and hands then she would have laughed at the picture he presented.

Then, the words sank into her head. Breeder? She didn't think so.

"Look, I'm sure you guys could show a girl a real fine time, but I have other plans tonight." When all else fails, smart-ass them. Bliss winced. She really didn't think it was going to work.

"She's a saucy one, Mordan," the tall, muscular creature that had blocked her moments before murmured softly. "She would make an excellent warrior. Not just a breeder."

"Neither is on my list of things to do this year," she retorted as she backed further away, aware that each step took her away from the bar and the chance of rescue.

"Only the breeding will be required," the leader assured her smoothly.

"Yeah, well, that's the one I have the most exception to." She stilled the tremor in her voice and in her knees. "Tell you what, check with me next year when my biological clock is getting closer to ticking. Maybe I will have changed my mind."

"By this time next year, you will have whelped and bled dry your first young and be growing heavy with the second," she was told coldly. "Breeders are chained in our cells, taken regularly, their used to strengthen our warriors. You will be a very fertile breeder. I can smell the ripeness of your body…"

"Damn, and here I showered and everything." This wasn't happening.

She danced just out of reach of the hand that shot out, intent on grabbing her close. The muttered curse assured her that they were quickly running out of patience. This had not been her week, she thought with hysterical humor. First, a horny vampire intent on breaking her heart and making her just like him, and now this.

"You know, this is really not fucking fair," she yelled at the three approaching monsters.

Yep, she would agree with Cadan now. Monsters really did exist.

They paused as though surprised she had dared to scream out her fury in such a way.

"Life was not meant to be fair," the one called Mordan observed.

"Fucking blood sucking philosopher—just what the hell I needed tonight. I wanted to get drunk. Dead dog puking drunk and you are messing up my plans. Do you hear me? I don't like this."

She hated having control taken from her, and she sure as hell didn't like being called a breeder or being informed of exactly what that entailed. She preferred to choose the father of her children herself, thank you very much. And if it was all the same to these blood sucking morons she wouldn't mind a bit if any children she had lived into old age rather than be killed by their mother. Not that she really believed that one, but the way her week was going, anything was possible.

"This mate your son has chosen does not seem very sane, Mordan. Is there not a chance of that insanity infecting the symbiot that would be bred from her?" the one on the end asked suspiciously.

"Insane?" she snapped backed. "I'm not insane, you are. I'm perfectly reasonable. I think this sucks. Do you have any idea how long it's been since I've been mad enough to get dog drunk? I don't like having it ruined."

Were they weak-minded or what? She stepped back further as the one called Mordan watched her carefully.

"Cadan would not choose for his mate one so weak as to be insane," he informed the others. "Smell her. She reeks of him. Even now his seed searches for fertile ground."

She trembled. "God, this is so unreal," she muttered as they began to progress again. "You are breaking the fucking rules. Every damned one of them. Dead people don't procreate. Vampires are not alive. This is not real."

Mordan reached for her again. Bliss let her scream shriek through the night. Hell, she had a healthy set of lungs, or so her father had always claimed. Surely someone would hear her.

"Let me go, you freak." Her shirt ripped as she tore herself loose from the fingers that snagged the material.

She ducked the next arm and took off running.

"Help me!" The night seemed to swallow her screams.

Chapter Twelve

For the first time in recent memory the street was deserted, the drunken fools normally laughing and falling all over themselves mysteriously absent. Bliss had taken no more than a few steps when she was caught from behind, a hand coming over her mouth as she opened her lips and bit down, hard. She screamed, scratched and clawed, kicking out with her feet and struggling violently as she was dragged back to the alley.

"You bastards. Sons of bitches. I'm going to get me a symbiot and fucking kick your asses. I'm going to rip your fucking balls from your bodies and shove them down your throats, you stupid rule breaking blood sucking creeps…"

She was still cursing when she was abruptly torn from the arms holding her and lifted against a hard, familiar chest. Laughter echoed in her ear, warm and inviting, as one strong arm circled her waist and held her firm.

"Bliss, baby, your language." Cadan laughed in amusement as her arms clawed at him, desperate to hold onto him and terrified that he was so well outnumbered that he couldn't possibly save her.

"Damn you," she cried against his chest. "I'm not a breeder. And I won't kill my babies, Cadan. And there aren't going to be any babies because I'm going to castrate every damned one of you."

She realized she was crying, sobbing against his chest as he held her close to him. Warmth surrounded her, not just in front of her but all around her now, as silence seemed to stretch throughout the street.

"I'm well fed, Father," Cadan said softly with an innate, curiously lethal danger that had her nerve endings fraying more than they were already. "Well fed and well defended. Would you prefer to fight another day?"

Bliss turned and stared at her would-be rapist in fury.

"That's your father?" she asked him, her breath hitching with her tears. "I have to tell you, Cadan, your family sucks. And not in a good way, either."

Cadan's laughter was low, brooding. "Meet my father, Mordan, my brother, the sloppy bleeder, Angus, and my uncle, Kiran." Kiran, of course, being the strange one who had doubted her sanity.

"It's not been a pleasure," she muttered, holding onto Cadan with a desperate grip.

"We will have her eventually, Cadan," his father warned him mockingly. "She may yet carry that female bitch Cerise, but that will not save her anymore than it saved the last host she possessed."

"Ahh, but there you are wrong," Cadan promised him lightly. "The last host didn't like feeding. I will ensure Bliss has no such problems. Imagine her, Father." His voice dropped, filled with humor, with triumph. "Cerise is one of the oldest, the strongest, as is Aldon. Well fed and healthy, they were the leaders for a reason. Bliss will know a power you can never comprehend. And she's perhaps just a bit irrational on top of that. She could sweep through your warriors like a plague and leave you lying in your own waste. That I am looking forward to in ways you can never imagine."

Okay, it sounded good, Bliss thought, restraining her shudder. Not realistic, but a hell of a threat.

Mordan snarled in fury. "Cerise is an insipid bitch. She can not defeat us."

"Not alone," Cadan agreed. "Not without her mate. But she has found her mate now. She and Aldon will only grow in strength. The host who shall shelter her is my woman. The power will grow, Father, our strength will be tenfold. Run. Run hard and run fast, because next time we meet, your blood will flow and vengeance will finally be mine. Both for myself and for my mother and sisters who loved you so unwisely. You will die."

Bliss could feel the hatred pouring from Cadan then. Black menace emanated from his hard body, swirled in the air like currents of electricity and snapped dangerously around them all.

"You guys are so melodramatic," she said, trying to still the tears of rage and fear. "You seriously need to chill out."

Mordan's gaze swung to her, his frown dark and promising retribution.

"I will cut your tongue from your mouth when I finally take you, bitch," he snarled. "You will be on your knees whimpering for mercy when I have finished with you."

Her fingernails dug into Cadan's waist, holding tightly to him, terrified that if she let go of him he might leave her to fend for herself.

"Or cutting off your tiny balls, you fruitcake," she snapped. "Don't you have things to do? Graves to dig or something? I thought vampires were smarter than this. Someone needs to give you guys lessons on how to do it right."

"She reads too many fiction novels." Cadan sighed. "I'm trying to break her of this habit."

His laughter soothed her, stroked over the terror-laced nerves and brought a measure of calm to her racing heart.

Mordan sneered before casting his son a dark, malevolent look then turning and stalking away. The brother followed closely behind, though the uncle stood silent, watching the scene with faint amusement.

"Do you think you can avoid the battle to come forever, nephew?" he asked curiously. "Mordan grows more powerful by the day and more angry. Allowing your woman to taunt him in such a way is foolhardy."

His voice was like a mellow spring, rippling with subtle power and wrapping around them now in a way it hadn't when the other two had been present.

"Watch your own back, Kiran, and I will watch mine," Cadan told him softly. "As long as you fight alongside my father, we are enemies. Nothing more."

"And yet, those who carry your blood have not shed a drop of it by your sword," Kiran said softly. "Something else stays your hand, nephew. Such foolishness could mean your death."

"And perhaps you see what you only choose to see," Cadan drawled with an edge of laughter. Did he never take anything seriously? "I will bid you goodnight now. I have a woman to prepare, and a symbiot shrieking in my head. And you might want to collect your dead on the next street over. I believe Father is now missing several of his warriors, as well as the symbiots who inhabited them. They're getting lazy in their feedings these days."

Kiran's eyes narrowed. He nodded abruptly then turned and strode quickly away, following the route the others had taken and leaving Cadan and Bliss alone with the night surrounding them.

"Well, that was interesting." She still hadn't let him go and she wasn't about to for a long while. "I have to say, though, your family doesn't impress me much, Cadan."

He breathed out deeply. "For this, I cannot blame you," he said wearily as both arms enfolded her. "I'm sorry you were frightened in such a way but I have to say, I did warn you."

"You would be an 'I told you so' type," she grunted as she felt his lips press against her hair.

He could say it all he wanted to as far as she was concerned, as long as he kept her wrapped in his arms, kept her sheltered from the terror of realizing everything he had told her was completely true.

"I am a realistic and very weary type," he finally told her. "And I must feed quickly, Bliss. I will take you to the bar…"

"No." She gripped his lean waist tighter. "Are you kidding me? There isn't a chance in hell I'm letting go of you. Those guys meant business, Cadan."

"I am well aware of this, Bliss, but I must feed. I cannot wait any longer or I will grow weak. Unless you're willing to watch, then we have no other choice. I promise it will not take long."

"Do you have to fuck them?" She remembered Marissa and jealousy blazed within her.

He chuckled gently. "No, dearest, I haven't taken another since you completed me that first night. But the act is still erotic, sensual. There is no hope for that. The adrenaline-laced blood is more powerful and lasts much longer than that which is taken from a body at rest. You will learn this yourself."

She felt his hands smoothing over her back as he spoke, attempting to calm the surge of emotion running through her.

"Why can't you just take my blood?" she whispered.

"Because, you must be strong, at your most healthy to accept the symbiot later. If I feed from you, it will weaken you. At the time of the bonding, we'll take blood from each other. And though that will be part of our sensuality, we always need to feed from others. There is no help for that."

"You wouldn't be jealous, watching me do that to another man?" She was barely aware of him leading her to the bar.

"I would never allow you to fuck another man, my love." His voice hardened a bit at the statement. "But watching you arouse him, feed from him, would make me mad to have you myself. Yes, that I could handle."

She could hear the arousal in his voice now.

"I want to watch." She tried to ignore the heat in her pussy at the thought of watching Cadan touch another woman. It was depraved. "For purely clinical purposes," she assured him. "I need to see how it's done before I decide if I can do it."

"Hmm." The soft sound of curious reflection was followed by a suspicious tremor in his chest.

She was certain he was laughing at her.

"No more little rips like Marissa, though," she told him. "She could be carrying nasty germs. Get someone clean at least."

"Clean, huh?" He cleared his throat. Yep, he was laughing at her. "Would you perhaps prefer to choose dinner for me?"

She grimaced at the description. "Might as well." She sighed. "Other than when you picked me, you've had lousy taste in women."

"Do you think so?" They entered the bar, standing close, staring around at the crowded room, listening to the cacophony of sound as Bliss tried to convince herself that she was indeed safe now.

"I know so." She breathed in deeply and patted his chest comfortingly. "Don't worry, honey, I'll pick you out a tasty little morsel. I have excellent taste in people. You'll see."

Chapter Thirteen

He had to agree she had excellent taste in choosing women. He wondered if that was a good thing, though.

The woman was a fiery redhead, small in stature, with full ripe breasts, though not nearly as fine as Bliss's were, he thought as he held her in thrall, his gaze locked with Bliss's as he bent his head to the woman's neck. There was no question that he would attempt to fuck the woman. Not that she wasn't well prepared. It had taken very little to arouse the seductive beauty. But Bliss's promise to cut his balls off if he attempted to fuck the woman still echoed in his head.

He licked at the graceful neck bent to him, watching his woman, seeing her eyes darken with arousal, curiosity. After preparing the flesh, his lips drew back, allowing her to see the slow lengthening of his canines, the tips becoming sharper, lethal.

The redhead was breathing heavier now, her nipples hardening beneath her shirt, her face flushing with arousal. Gently, careful to allow Bliss to see every move, he sank his teeth into the tender vein awaiting him.

The redhead orgasmed. He watched Bliss's eyes narrow as she caught the betraying shudder, heard the thick pleasure in the moan that whispered from lipsticked lips. Then his own lips covered the small wound as he began to draw the spicy fluid into his mouth.

His cock was harder now than it had been the first two times he had taken Bliss. He couldn't believe the lust she inspired in him. Just watching her, seeing the hunger in her expression, the excitement in her eyes, made him crazy to fuck her. That need transmitted through the psychic link that connected him to the redhead, making her shift in his arms, her body to rub against his in renewed passion.

The redhead's blood simmered with her lust. He could taste the excitement, feel it flowing through his body, replacing the blood that the symbiots slowly drained from him daily. It was an interesting process. One he had studied for years and still didn't fully understand. He could feel it, though. Sliding over his tongue, down his throat, then tingling through his cells, moving into his veins, replacing weariness with extraordinary power, recharging his body.

But the lust Bliss was filling him with was just as potent. He had never known anything quite like this. Watching her, seeing her desires, feeling her need to experience what the woman in his arms felt, her hunger to taste him as well. His muscles clenched at the sensation, his erection pulsing with the need to fill her once again.

"Cadan." Bliss whispered his name beseechingly as he slowly drew his lips from the redhead's neck, feeling her slump weakly in his arms, sleep overcoming her as he lowered her to the couch beside him.

"Get out of here," he growled, knowing if he touched her, neared her, he would be unable to keep himself from taking her blood. He could feel the powerful fluid flowing through her veins, calling to him, whispering seductively of a taste unlike any other, a power that he would never know otherwise.

"I can't," she whispered, leaning against the wall, her breathing harsh, labored. "I've never known anything like this, Cadan. What's wrong with me?

He stopped, containing his arousal.

Cerise, he screamed within his mind. *What the fuck are you up to?*

Me? Cerise questioned him harshly. *It's all I can do to stay in place, Cadan. She's calling to me. Feel her. Hear her. She needs me; her mind and her soul are demanding my presence. Release me now.*

Desperation filled her thoughts. *Now, Cadan, or it may be too late. Release me.*

He stared back at Bliss, seeing the glitter in her eyes, the hunger that transformed her expression, made her appear exotic, ethereal, impossible to resist.

"Bliss." He moved to her quickly, picking her up in his arms as he carried her swiftly from the billiards room, up the stairs and into the private rooms that Walker sometimes loaned to important guests.

He locked the door quickly behind them then laid her on the bed, moving beside her as he pushed her hair from her face, watching her carefully.

"Stop," he told her, his heart breaking in ways he hadn't imagined possible. "You're calling to the symbiot, Bliss. I cannot force her to stay inside me if you keep doing so."

She licked her lips slowly, her eyelids lowering with sensual promise.

"I can do this," she whispered. "I feel it, Cadan. I need this. Let her go."

Elation surged inside him.

"Damn you," he whispered. "Be certain, Bliss. Be very certain. You can never go back. You can never change your mind."

"You can never leave me," she said softly. "We're bound. We are, aren't we, Cadan? I can feel it."

He could feel it. The bonding. The drawing of two souls...soul mates.

"I can never leave you," he promised her gently. "I can never take another, nor can you. I can never harm you, can never see you harmed. We're entwined, Bliss. This is love. This is what we have both searched for. Longed for."

Her smile was radiant.

"You get to bite me now," she whispered, relaxing beneath him. "Let me have her, Cadan. Let me share this world with you."

There was no stopping Cerise. He felt the wrenching, the soul tightening feel of her pulling from his mind and body, and watched the shimmer of brilliant light as it began to leave him.

Bliss's eyes widened a second later. Pure joy filled her expression as Cerise's form settled over her, head to toes, a bright shimmer of color that slowly dissolved into Bliss's body.

Her back bowed, her body tightened, shuddered and for one long, heart stopping moment she moaned with exquisite pain that he knew bordered ecstasy.

It didn't take long. It never took females long to bond, he knew. Their acceptance, their grace and understanding made them the easiest symbiot sex to absorb. Males were painful to accept, the bonding process a blinding stroke of agony that came much too close to death.

Long minutes later, her eyes opened. The once pretty shade of green had intensified, deepened, filled now with the power and vibrancy of the energy form that shared her body.

"They are mates," she whispered. "Cerise and Aldon, your symbiot. Did you know they were mates, Cadan? Unable to touch, unable to bond because their hosts were not mates as well?"

He had suspected it.

"They are together now," he whispered. "Just as we are, Bliss. Forever. Together."

"Forever," she agreed, touching his cheek softly as she relaxed against his larger body. "Forever."

Chapter Fourteen
Two Weeks Later

He had created a monster. Not the type he needed to kill, but the type that would definitely kill him. Kill him with desire, with frustration, with sheer joy.

Cadan sat back on the couch, stroking his cock slowly as he watched the male attend to his woman. Bliss was laid back across the long coffee table, her legs held wide as the man lapped and sucked at her now hairless pussy.

It was glistening with her juices, plump and swollen with her arousal as the man sucked at her clit, licked at the silken folds of skin or tongue fucked her deep and hard as she cried out her need.

Of course, the puny-dicked little man wasn't ever going to fuck her, Cadan would make certain of that. But watching him arouse Bliss, seeing his lips and tongue paint her body had been incredibly erotic. Watching as the man's mouth prepared her tight little pussy for Cadan's thick cock had been even more exciting.

"Cadan, when?" Bliss was panting, hungry. Her lethal canines had dropped from her gums as the sexual tension flamed within her body.

"Soon," he promised her gently, watching as two long fingers penetrated her pussy and pushed inside her. "In a minute, baby."

She moaned at the refusal to allow her to feed immediately.

"I can't stand it. At least don't watch. Let me catch my breath."

It made her wild when he watched. Made her go to lengths he was certain she would have never gone to on her own. It made her brave, daring, free. His woman. Never had he thought he would find a woman who met life head-on and found the same exhilaration he did in each day lived.

She was a treasure to him. She was his heart, his very soul.

A low, feminine growl brought him out of his thoughts and back to the sight of her being pleasured by another. Her cunt had flowered open; like silken petals the folds of flesh had become swollen, parting, revealing satiny-pink skin slick with the essence of her lust.

Her head was thrown back as she raced for release now, her lips parting over the sharp canines that had grown from her gums. The man pleasuring her was wrapped in his own fantasy of lust, unaware that he would never actually plunge his dick inside the hot channel his fingers were stroking, stretching. He would soon be beneath her delicate body, her teeth at his throat as Cadan himself took the honor of fucking her into a mind-blowing orgasm.

"Thomas, lay down for her now," Cadan ordered the pussy-feasting male.

At the order, the lanky male went to his back on the floor, his cock standing at full mast, gleaming wetly with his pre-seminal fluids. Bliss didn't wait for Cadan to give her permission to go to the man. Within seconds, she was straddling his body, his dick pressing against his lower stomach as she cushioned it against the pad of her hot pussy.

Cadan groaned at the sight of his woman bending over the other man. His cock twitched as he rose from the couch, moving to her spread thighs and the fiery cunt he so loved to fuck.

"Gently, beloved," he instructed her as her mouth caressed the neck that had been bared to her. "Hold off just a second longer. Let your own passions soar and he will feel your excitement, you pleasure, as though it were his own. It is then that you want to begin."

He knew her symbiot would be doing her part to hold Bliss back, to tutor her in the ways of feeding just as she tutored her host in the ways of fighting. If needed, she would take control of Bliss and restrain her mentally, ensuring that neither the male beneath her, nor Bliss, would know any harm from the experience.

He could feel his symbiot connecting with the female, bonding with her on their unique plane as Cadan prepared to bond with Bliss on the physical.

He ran the thick head of his cock through the heavy juices that covered her gleaming pussy. She was hot, so soft, so beckoning that he grimaced with the effort it took to hold back and not slam inside her.

"Tease me and I'll make you pay." Her voice was rich with hunger, with throbbing need. "Fuck me, damn you. I won't break."

She was panting now, and as Cadan watched he saw her sweet juices drip from her pussy to the heavy balls of the man beneath her. It was too much. Bliss wasn't the only one walking the fine line of an overpowering lust.

Cadan gripped her hips in his hands, his cock lodged at the entrance of her pussy, and tried to take her gently. She was still so tiny, so damned tight around his thick flesh that he feared hurting her.

"Now," she begged breathlessly, her head moving restlessly as her lips and tongue caressed the man's strong throat. "Fuck me, Cadan. Fuck me hard and deep. Make me take it all."

His breath was expelled from his throat as he groaned roughly at the plea. He didn't want to hurt her. Didn't want to shatter the trust that built between them.

"Easy, Bliss," he groaned, beginning to work inside her slowly, closing his eyes against the incredible pleasure of her tight pussy.

"No," she cried out, and before Cadan could halt her, could move back to lessen the effect of her movement, her hips had slammed backward, her pussy swallowing every hard, engorged inch of his pulsing cock.

She stole his control, stole his breath and replaced it with a pleasure he could have never imagined. He was aware of her fangs sinking into the throat beneath her, the hot, rich flow of blood into her strong body, the lust thickening around them, and the muscles of her cunt milking him as he gripped her hips tighter and began to thrust hard and deep inside her. Exquisite heat, electricity and primal sensation washed through him in ever increasing waves. It slammed into his body, into his brain, overpowered everything he was and every preconceived notion of pleasure he had ever had. This was paradise.

* * * * *

Bliss would have screamed if the driving hunger inside her body had allowed it. The abrupt shock of his wide cock searing past the sensitive muscles of her cunt sent her spiraling into an ecstasy she couldn't attempt to fight. It was in that moment that Cerise demanded she sink her teeth into Thomas's blood-rich vein. It was pumping with lust, with lush pleasure, as he believed his cock was caught in the hot grip of her pussy as he pumped his way to release.

The erotic taste of the lust-rich blood was intoxicating, powerful, fueling her own passions and her pleasure until she existed in a sensuous, ecstatic haze that she had no desire to escape.

Behind her, Cadan was fucking her with deep, hard, jackhammer strokes that pushed her closer to the brink, threw her into the maelstrom of eroticism and had her reaching, reaching…

Her head lifted from Thomas's throat, the little pinpricks instantly closing as the flow of blood out of the vein halted. Her head pressed against his shoulder, her hips raising, pushing back to the driving force possessing her as she allowed the pleasure to overtake her.

Sensation whipped through her body like electricity gone wild, zapping into her clitoris, her womb, convulsing her pussy as it rippled around Cadan's driving cock until she exploded.

Light shimmered behind her closed eyelids, brilliant fire bursts of color and carnal bliss that blasted into her in violent waves of exquisite sensual gratification. The earth moved. The mountains shuddered...or she did. She wasn't certain. All she knew was the violent release quaking through her body and the hard, hot spurts of Cadan's seed filling her pussy.

Bliss collapsed over Thomas, her body strong and powerful, yet weak with the release of her pleasure. Her symbiot had sent the psychic demand to Thomas that he needed to sleep now, to rest. That his pleasure had been extreme and his body well satisfied.

Behind her, Cadan breathed harshly, and inside her, his cock twitched with the last tremors of release. They were adrift now on clouds of enchanting fulfillment, within a connection so deep that she could touch his heart, his soul, and know the passion and love that only grew daily.

"Come on, woman." He moved back slowly, groaning as his cock slid from the tight clasp of her pussy. "Bedtime."

They were both weary. Mordan hadn't given up in his fight to take Bliss and use her for his own evil purposes, and the battles were now being fought nightly. The only light in the darkness of the battles was the symbiots they had rescued from the dark warriors. They now awaited within the few life capsules that Cadan had found over the centuries.

Cadan lifted her into his arms, sheltering her against his chest as he carried her to the bed. After he tucked her in, he would awaken Thomas, prepare him a light meal and then send him on his way. Cadan took care of her like that. Sheltered her, loved her. Her blood sucking playboy stud was hers alone now. His heart, his soul, his body. Just as she was his.

He laid her back in the bed, pulled the blankets over her body and kissed her lips softly.

"Sleep well, beloved," he told her gently before dressing and moving from the room.

Bliss watched him with drowsy eyes, a smile curving her mouth.

You'll never tame that wild man, Cerise thought to her with an edge of amusement. *He's still a stud.*

But he's our stud, Bliss informed her with a smile.

Yes, our stud, Cerise agreed.

Cerise moved within the power that connected her to her mate. The bond Cadan and Bliss had formed was strong, vibrant. A pure, intense love that allowed Cerise to touch Aldon often, to experience through her host the touch, the feel of the mate she had longed for all these centuries.

Sleep, beloved, Aldon whispered to her mind, his presence a comfort that stilled the pain she had known for too long.

The bond filled her with warmth, with a glowing strength she had not known since the deaths of their mated hosts nearly a thousand years before on the planet they had once called home. It was good, Cerise thought, to be a part of him once again.

* * * * *

As Bliss slipped finally into deep sleep, a similar thought lingered within her mind. She was a part of that something more she had always dreamed of. Strong and free, sheltered and loved and yet trusted to do her part. She was, for the first time in her life, complete.

About the author:

Lora welcomes mail from readers. You can write to her c/o Ellora's Cave Publishing at 1337 Commerce Drive, Suite 13, Stow OH 44224.

Also by Lora Leigh:

* books in print

DEVILISH DOT
A KHAN-GOR TALE
FROM THE TREK MI Q'AN SERIES

Jaid Black

To Dot...

You're funny and passionate, generous and outrageous, affectionate and tender-hearted. You give to others freely, never asking for anything for yourself in return. What you haven't figured out yet is just how special you are to so many, and how many smiles you bring into an otherwise dreary day to women the world over. Thank you for being my friend.

Love Always, Jaid

Chapter One
Rural California
Present Day

She loved sex. Lots and lots of sweaty, pumping, pounding, gloriously wicked, undeniably naughty, kinky as all hell S-E-X with a capital S for *Sex*.

It didn't matter where she was—even driving along the highway in her very unsexy clunker of a car, the mere thought of impending passion made Dorothy "Dot" Araiza's pulse race. It made her doe-brown eyes grow heavy-lidded and her legs squeeze together. It made her hands clench into tight fists and her breath catch in the back of her throat.

(Confused passersby on the interstates might have mistaken her arousal for seizures a time or two, but oh well.)

Yes, Dot loved sex. There was no denying that fact of life. It was just too bad she wasn't getting any, she thought with a snarl. Because maybe if she was, she wouldn't be sitting in her car, driving through a torrential downpour, voluntarily giving up her Friday night to sell her toys at a bachelorette party.

Dot's nostrils flared as she stepped on the gas pedal and plowed through the back roads of the one-horse bumpkin town like nobody's business. She'd never even heard of Nowhere, California, for Pete's sake! It certainly wasn't on the map. But work was work and if this Nowhere existed, well hell, she'd find it.

Dot supposed being a sex toy maker had its distinct advantages. She got to work from home. She enjoyed the thrill of invention. And, she thought on a harrumph that could rival any bah-humbug by Ebenezer Scrooge, the local charities never hit her up at Christmas for donations to the *Toyz For Tots* fund. One look at what kind of toys she made and all bets were off.

Her former shrink had once told her she loved sex so much because in her mind it was a replacement for affection. An infliction that mostly males suffered from, but which strikes the occasional female. If that was true, Dot supposed she was a human lightning rod.

She often fantasized about being swept off her feet by an extremely tall, muscular, hunky, alpha male kind of guy. He would snatch her up and gently but demandingly throw her onto her elegant pink satin bed with all its lace and ruffles. And then—oh boy and then!—he would, to be blunt, fuck the shit out of her. Oh yeah, Dot thought with a small smile, she entertained that fantasy a lot.

The problem with turning fantasy into reality was that, as much as she loved sex, Dot also had the distinct disadvantage of being rather, well—shy. Very shy, unfortunately. Wallflower shy, she thought through gritted teeth. Wallflower, hopeless, sexless, utterly pathetic kind of shy. *Arrrg!* The minute a man so much as glanced in her direction she was all babbling idiot and no action.

Dot thought back on the last time she'd almost done the horizontal mambo and couldn't help but to grimace. Henry had been far from tall, not at all muscular, and nowhere in the vicinity of being an alpha male. The extremely conservative and rather butt-ugly pharmacist with the perpetually running nose might not have been a hunk or even close to it, but he'd been able to put her at ease enough to talk to him. Not even a woman so shy as she was could continue to babble like an idiot rather than carry on a half-intelligent conversation with a man as harmless as Henry.

And so they'd gone out. Once. Twice. Three times. By the time the tenth date rolled around and the pharmacist had made no move to bed her, Dot feared they'd never get down to business and have sex. So she'd set out to seduce Henry. What a disaster that had turned out to be!

Dot had read in a men's magazine that males really go for forward women, that they love it when their woman seizes the moment and jumps their bones. If that was the case, she thought, her hands gripping the steering wheel until her knuckles turned white, the author of that column had clearly never met Henry.

She had donned that see-through, peek-a-boo, pink satin nightie of hers which perfectly coordinated with the pink satin draped across her bed. Slipping into her matching pair of high heels, she picked up "Diesel-Dirk" — the name she'd given to the 30-speed ten-inch vibrator she'd designed and patented herself — and sashayed into the living room of her modest home-cum-laboratory where Henry had been patiently waiting on her to get ready for yet another date at the local frozen yogurt parlor.

The sound of Henry blowing his nose into the stained, moist hankie that always accompanied him like an appendage didn't deter her. The fact that she was two inches taller (six inches in heels) and about twenty pounds heavier didn't matter in that moment. She let down her chestnut-brown hair from its confining bun, shook it out until it cascaded down her back in soft waves, took a deep breath as she regally thrust her chin up and breasts out, and continued her seductive walk into the living room.

"Hello Henry," Dot had breathed out in a practiced, sultry voice. Henry had stilled as she came to a halt before him, his eyes widening and his jaw dropping. His expression made her confidence falter for a brief second, but recalling an old Mae West line she plowed on determinedly. "Is that a gun in your pocket," she asked in a Marilyn Monroe whisper, "or are you happy to see me?"

His face chalk-white and his eyes unblinking, Henry had then proceeded to pull out two very used hankies from his pocket and lay them on the coffee table, his deer-caught-in-headlights expression never wavering. Dot had frowned. That hadn't been the reaction she'd been going for.

You were supposed to say you are happy to see me, idiot! Now what do I do!

Her heart began pounding against her breasts. Her brown eyes rounded in embarrassment and horror. She hesitated for a moment before taking a calming breath and regaining her original level of confidence.

Plowing onward, she took "Diesel-Dirk" out from behind her back. She smiled as she held up the long, thick, veined vibrator that was, if she did say so herself, the perfect imitation of a well-endowed African-American man's cock. "Dirk has given me pleasure beyond my wildest dreams," she said in that smoky voice she'd practiced for ages. "Let him give you pleasure, too, Henry."

What she'd meant by that statement was she wanted to use Dirk on herself for Henry's viewing pleasure. Apparently Henry had thought Dot meant to screw him up the butt with it for not even five seconds later, the pharmacist had gasped, eyes rolling into the back of his head, as he'd fainted dead away.

Arrrg!

Needless to say, the night had only gone downhill from there. She'd spent the next hour reviving and re-reviving a frightened, stuttering Henry. Within thirty seconds of being able to stand upright on two shaking feet, he'd ran from Dot's house as though she'd sprouted horns and spewed green venom at him.

That, she thought, nostrils flaring and jaw tight as she drove down the back road through the pouring rain, had been the last time she'd had sex. Or almost had sex. That was four years ago now. Actual penetration with a member of the male species had last occurred four years before that.

The memory of *that* night was even worse than the Henry fiasco.

"Men suck!" Dot wailed into the night, yelling at everybody and nobody. "Who needs you anyway. I've got my toys!"

And oh boy did she have toys. If there was one thing Dot knew she could do better than anybody else, it was create the perfect sex toys for sexually frustrated females. Being one of those women, well, she'd managed to turn her hobby into a full-time job.

There was "Freddy-The-Fish", a male mouth that could suck a woman blind. "Cum-Hither-Kenny", a 20-speed vibrator with interchangeable heads that could do everything but make you breakfast. And, of course, there was good ole Dirk—still her most popular seller. Dirk could not only make you scream like a banshee in heat, but he was also capable of screwing you— hands free!—when mounted on a special mechanism she'd designed solely for the purpose of a woman being able to get off without having to hold the vibrator steady in her hands.

Dot reached over to the passenger seat and affectionately petted Dirk on the crown of his glorious black head. "I just want to get this damn bachelorette party over and done with," she muttered, "then me and you will go home and have a little fun."

Who needed a real man, Dot decided on down-turned lips. She had Dirk. And Kenny. And—and…

Shit!

Dot screamed as a bolt of lightning illuminated the nighttime sky and cracked down in front of her car, effectively scaring the daylights out of her. Reacting instead of thinking, she veered a sharp left and before she knew what had happened her small sedan was in a flat-spin on a rainy, muddy back road.

"Oh my God!" Dot cried out, her heart racing and her eyes wide. She couldn't get control of the car. "Somebody help me!"

It was too late. She espied the tree a moment before the sedan made impact.

Her eyes rolling back and slowly flickering shut, she saw a flash of white and then nothing else.

Chapter Two
Hunting Grounds of the Zyon Pack
Planet Khan-Gor ("Planet of the Predators")
Seventh Dimension, 6078 Y.Y. (Yessat years)

Two crimson eyes flew open. Air rushed into depleted lungs, his concaved, translucent silver chest rapidly expanding to its total musculature and size. Deadly fangs exploded from his gums. Lethal claws and talons shot out from his fingers and toes.

She is near…

He had been cocooned for one hundred earth years, his body and mind in *gorak*—the Khan-Gori term for "the sleep of the dead". *Gorak* comes every five hundred Yessat Years and occurs between each of a Barbarian's seven lives. Five hundred and one Yessat Years he had spent without *her*, without the one. He mayhap ended his first life in defeat of finding her, but his second life was about to commence—

Vaidd Zyon could feel her, could sense her, could smell her. He took a slow, deep breath, nostrils flaring and eyes briefly closing, as he inhaled her scent.

It *was* her.

His Bloodmate.

He had evolved in *gorak*. Stronger. Deadlier. More ferocious than ever he was in his first life. 'Twas time to begin his second lifetime.

Every day, every hour, every second of the five hundred and one Yessat Years he'd spent without her had been akin to the blackest abyss. No sense of hope. No sense of joy. No reason to wish to evolve in *gorak* and begin the next five hundred years without the one who had been born that she might complete him. Many a day Vaidd had felt like ending it—forever.

But his pack needed him. Verily, he was his sire's heir apparent. And so he'd carried on. Grim. Lethal. Merciless. But he'd carried on.

Vaidd took another deep breath and, once more, inhaled the scent of his Bloodmate. She was close. Very close.

The beating of his heart stilled for one angry, possessive moment when his senses confirmed something else:

She was not alone. Other males drew near.

A low growl rumbled in his throat until it turned into a deafening roar. In an explosion of violence, hunger, possession, and desire, Vaidd burst from his cocoon and shot into the air, his twelve-foot wings expanding on a predator's ruthless cry. The instinct to return to his pack was overridden by the more primal need to track his Bloodmate—and kill any male that might touch her.

Her scent was strong, intoxicating. Bewitching. She *would* be his and no other's.

She belonged to him.

*　*　*　*　*

Dot's eyelids blinked in rapid succession as she slowly, groaningly, came to. Her forehead wrinkled in incomprehension as she glanced around. "Well hell's goddamn bells," she muttered. "Where in the world am I?"

What a night! she thought tragically. Turning off the engine, she opened the door of her car and arose from the driver's seat. The rain must have ended and brought a thick fog with a cold front in its stead, for she could barely see anything at all and felt so chilled to the bone that it was as if she'd woken up in the middle of the Arctic.

Frowning, she narrowed her eyes and ran her hands up and down her goose-pimpled arms, trying to make heads or tails of her location. But the fog was thick. She couldn't see anything at all other than what was in the immediate vicinity of her car. Not even with the headlights still shining off into the distance. What she thought the oddest, however, was that the tree she had collided with was no longer anywhere to be seen. But she'd definitely struck it...

Immediately noting that the oak she'd made impact with had left a highly noticeable dent in the driver's side door, she angrily slammed the thing shut and harrumphed. Feeling in true drama-queen form, she lifted the back of her hand up to her forehead and sighed.

Great! This is just terrific! I haven't had almost-sex in four years, actual sex in eight years, I spent my Friday night driving through a horrible rainstorm in the middle of nowhere trying to find Nowhere...and now on top of everything else, my insurance premium will go through the roof!

A lesser woman wouldn't be able to pull herself together, she thought on a sniff. A lesser woman would come undone.

Dot decided she was a lesser woman.

A warbled cry of anger, frustration—no doubt partially sexual in origin!—and dismay began in her belly, gurgled up to her throat, and exploded from her mouth in a shrill, shrieking cry. She kicked the door in three times for good measure with the toe of one of the black high-heeled shoes she wore. (The ones that perfectly coordinated with her pink suit ensemble, if she did say so herself.) Might as well. The damn door would need fixed anyway!

That accomplished, she screamed again, this time longer and louder. She jumped up and down like a mad jack-in-the-box as she shrieked, fists tight and nostrils flaring. Her hair came undone out of the tight bun she'd had it coiled in, but it didn't matter. Her tantrum was making her feel better. Much better, in fact.

A low growl pierced the quiet of the night. And then another. The growls sounded as if off from a distance, but growing closer by the millisecond.

Dot immediately shut-up. She ceased jumping. Her ears perked up and her eyes widened as she looked around.

Nothing.

The fog was so thick and all-encompassing that she couldn't see anything. And the growling had just altogether stopped — practically as soon as it had begun. She swallowed a bit roughly, wondering to herself if this was what people meant by the old colloquialism, "the quiet before the storm".

Dot hastily arrived at the conclusion that she didn't want to know.

Deciding she could finish up being a lesser woman later — like in the safety of her home! — the sex toy maker determined it would, perhaps, be in her best interests to get the hell out of dodge. Like now.

What a night! What a night! What a night!

Throwing open the door of her gray sedan, Dot quickly scurried into the vehicle, slammed the dented thing shut, and locked all the doors. Her eyes still wide, she nervously glanced around to try and ascertain if any wild animals were drawing near.

The growls. They are getting closer…

Her heartbeat picking up in tempo, she mentally chastised herself for reacting like a scared ninny while simultaneously turning the key and revving up the engine. No wild animal could get into a locked car! She knew that, yet an eerie feeling persisted just the same. She felt as if she was being — well…hunted.

No doubt her imagination, but she supposed it was best to err on the side of caution.

"Come on, Dot," she mumbled to herself. "Calm down. You can do this."

Problem was, the fog was as thick as clichéd pea soup. No matter how hard she squinted, she couldn't make out where she was let alone where she was going.

The eerie feeling grew, swamping her senses. She began to drive slowly, aimlessly, forward.

Light ahead! There is light just up ahead!

Dot stepped harder on the gas pedal, determinedly driving toward the faint illumination she could just barely make out in the distance. A small, brief smile of relief shown on her lips. The light was red — it had to mean a traffic signal or something of that nature. Civilization!

But as she drove out of the all-encompassing fog and into the dark, yet visible world that awaited her, it wasn't civilization that greeted her. At least not any sort of civilization she'd ever seen.

Dot's heart stilled as she loosed up on the gas pedal and came to a jarring stop. Dumbfounded, her jaw dropped. Her mind raced, inducing dizziness.

Well, Dorothy, you aren't in Kansas anymore. What the…?

Ice-capped mountains with razor-sharp tips surrounded her on all sides. It was cold here, so terribly, hypothermia-inducing frigid. Her current location seemed to be in a semi-forested valley of sorts between two of the mountains. *Translucent silver trees??* And the red illumination —

Dot gasped as she looked up. Her doe-brown eyes rounded to the shape of the four crimson moons she was gaping up at. Four moons. Four RED moons!

Blinking out of the trance-like state that had engulfed her, she held a palm to her forehead and whimpered. Either she was in a coma in some intensive care unit having one hell of a delusional dream or that last orgasm Dirk had given her had blown her mind — literally.

"Wake up, Dot," she whispered, her unblinking eyes staring up at the four crimson moons. "This isn't happening."

A lightning-fast movement caught her attention from out of her peripheral vision. Frightened, her heart skipped a beat as her head whiplashed to the right to see what that movement had been caused by. She sucked in a breath.

A man. A *naked* man. A naked man with…with…pearly white skin, black eyes, and a—holy shit! He/It had a tail!

Dirk — arrg! What have you done to me?

And then there was another. And another. And another. And another.

Dot's heart slammed in her chest as five of these…these— things—had her small, gray sedan surrounded. All five looked hungry, practically drooling as they took in the sight of her. They wanted to eat her, she hysterically thought. They were gazing at her like sushi.

"Oh my God!"

Screaming, Dot floored the gas pedal in an effort to outrace the creatures. Beads of perspiration broke out on her forehead and between her breasts as she frantically drove to anywhere.

Faster! Faster!

She drove aimlessly forward, not caring where the path led to so long as it didn't lead to any more of those things. But the men-beasts were bone-chillingly fast. Taking to all fours, they followed her. And—*oh God!*—caught up with her. Eighty miles an hour and they had caught up to her!

Dot's throat issued a final blood-curdling shriek for help as the creatures attacked the car, one jumping onto the hood and hissing while another pulled off the driver's side door to the sedan on a hungry growl.

Help me! Oh God — somebody help me!

Chapter Three

It didn't take the creatures long to overpower her. The car veered and swerved, Dot's mind too hysterical to scream, too frightened to do anything but try and regain control of the sedan.

This isn't happening! What are these things?

Men with tails. Black, fathomless eyes, white skin, hugely aroused dicks, and…tails! Out of all the horror and incredulity of the situation, it was the tails that she couldn't seem to work past. They looked like something out of an extremely weird (but highly creative) writer's imagination.

The creature that had managed to pull the driver's side door clean off the hinges was the biggest of the bunch. Huge, in fact. He had to stand in the vicinity of six and a half to seven feet tall. And sweet lord did he look hungry. Oh God! She didn't even want to contemplate what would happen to her if the beast-man managed to get her out of the sedan. Sushi-city.

Not even ten seconds later, nightmare became reality when, on a growl, the leader of the pack of creatures snatched Dot straight out of the car and into his awaiting arms. Screaming, she paled to a shade of white that could almost rival that of the beast-man's coloring.

"Let me go!" she cried, tears welling in her eyes as she beat her comparatively tiny fists against his naked chest. Blood pounded in her ears. Her heart was racing so fast she felt close to hyperventilating. *"OhmyGodOhmyGodOhmy –"*

Dot let out a yelp as the creature let her drop to the ground and onto her butt. She quickly shuffled up to her knees, her eyes round, her long, light brown hair tangled and disheveled.

"Please," she whimpered, her teeth chattering. "Don't kill me." She was freezing cold, but the adrenaline kept her insides warm. From somewhere deep down inside she found the courage to look up, to meet the leader of this pack of things in the eye. He didn't seem to comprehend what she was saying — or care to understand it. His pupil-less black gaze made it impossible to determine that; it was the strange way he'd cocked his head that had made her realize he couldn't understand a word she'd said. And yet again, against all hope, she softly begged, "Please…"

Within the blink of an eye, all five of the creatures were on her, forcing her to her feet and tearing at her clothes. She tried to run, but again they pounced, easily catching her and eagerly ripping her pink suit and undergarments from her body until she was totally naked. The beast-men dragged her — kicking, naked, and screaming — from out of the icy valley and into a nearby cave.

"Help meeeeeee!" she wailed. *"Please somebody help meeeeeeee!"*

Fear the likes of which Dot had never before known engulfed her. Either these things wanted to rape her or they'd shredded her clothes to bits because it made devouring her flesh easier. Each scenario — or worse *both* scenarios — were equally distressing.

Her heartbeat raced so fast that dizziness consumed her. Perspiration once again broke out on her forehead and between her breasts. Ice-cold terror lanced through her as the five male creatures forced her to the ground and pinned her to it.

Earlier in the evening, Dot had succumbed to fainting because she'd experienced what she assumed was a temporary concussion. This time she thankfully, mercifully, fainted out of fear. Her last memory before unconsciousness took over was of her legs being harshly spread apart…and of a male head diving between her legs. Of all the places to dine on her flesh —

Just let me pass out! Oh thank you, God, for letting me faint…

* * * * *

Vaidd Zyon heard his Bloodmate's screams echo throughout the mountains. Anger and possessiveness, mingled with terror at the thought of losing his *vorah* before he'd even found her, made his already swift wings swoop up and down all the faster. A merciless growl rumbled up from his throat, his fangs and talons visible and ready to kill.

He could not lose her—would not lose her. Without her...

He chose not to contemplate it. There was, for any evolved male of learned dimensions, but one. Only *one* female who could complete him, who could bare his offspring, whose mind and soul could meld with his.

'Twas said the warriors of Trek Mi Q'an knew naught but darkness and hopelessness without the finding of their mate. Verily, a Khan-Gori male knew seven lifetimes whereas a warrior knew but one—'twas naught worse than seven lifetimes spent in darkness and defeat.

His Bloodmate was still several hundred miles off. It could take a few hours to reach her. Mayhap she'd encountered a sentinel and found herself at its mercy. Mayhap—

Vaidd frowned when his acute senses picked up the scent of the males causing his *vorah* to screech. Verily, he couldn't fathom her fright. 'Twas but a pack of harmless, hungry male yenni! Why fear weak creatures such as those? It made no sense.

Unless...

Vaidd's heart all but stopped for a moment when he realized his Bloodmate was not of this galaxy, not even of this dimension. He'd been so intoxicated with need and aroused by her scent that it never once occurred to him 'twas the scent of a female primitive bewitching him. This explained his Bloodmate's fear of the yenni. She harbored no knowledge of what they were or of how they fed.

His already aroused cock swelled impossibly harder, longer, and thicker. He had heard tales of what 'twas like to bed a primitive. Verily, a male he knew from another pack had claimed one as his Bloodmate. So heady were the tales that before Vaidd had gone into the sleep of the dead, he'd been told by members of his own pack that they were planning a scouting party to primitive, first-dimension earth to look for their *vorahs*.

'Twas said a primitive female could nigh unto suck a Barbarian blind — and ruthlessly fuck him in the bed furs. 'Twas also said that, unlike females of this dimension, primitives were harder to tame.

Vaidd absently licked his fangs as he considered the reality that was his. Five hundred and one Yessat Years he'd spent without his one. But the gods and goddesses had smiled down upon him whilst he was in *gorak*.

A primitive. A female primitive.

And she was *his*.

* * * * *

Dot gasped, semi-regaining consciousness on a hard orgasm.

"Dirk?" she whimpered, groggy eyelids fluttering open as her breathing grew labored. She moaned as her large nipples hardened, the areolas jutting up into stiff, pink points.

No — not Dirk. Freddy-The-Fish. Yes. Yes, of course.

Duh! she thought, her eyelids fanning shut on a dreamy smile. How could she have not recognized the realistic feel of the very cunnilingus toy she'd created with her own two hands?

Slurp. Slurp. Slurp. Sluuuuuuuuuurrrrrrrrrrp.

Dot frowned. She couldn't recall Freddy ever being able to make sounds with his mouth. A worthy idea, she mentally conceded. Perhaps the newer model she was working on could...

She stilled. Memories jolted through her.

A car crash. Fog. Icy mountains. Bone-chilling coldness. Four crimson moons. Man-things with big dicks — and tails!

Her eyelids flew open on a soft cry, her brown gaze traveling down her body — and between her legs. "Holy shit," she mumbled.

They were down there. All five of those…those — *things*. And they were lapping at her pussy juice like it was a meal or something.

Her heart began to race. Her breasts heaved up and down.

On a groan, Dot slapped a palm to her forehead. "I've lost it!" she wailed. She grimly wondered if the losing of one's mind was a fate common to any woman who hadn't been almost-laid in four years and totally laid in eight. She had given up on finding a man so now her delusional brain was creating fictional males for her — five of them no less!

But what the hell is with the tails!?

Dot decided that *that* particular aspect of the delusion had to be Freudian in nature. Perhaps she shouldn't have dumped her shrink so quickly after all.

But this feels so real…

A low, warning growl issued from one of the males. Dot's forehead wrinkled. She recognized that male. He was the one she had, for some reason, thought of as the leader of the pack of creatures when she'd first encountered them.

And, indeed, he was. At his growl, the other four males whimpered and scampered away from Dot's body while the biggest of the beast-men continued lapping at her pussy, licking up all her juices. Her breathing grew impossibly heavier. Torn between fear and arousal, she didn't know what to do. She didn't even know if this was real. It just couldn't be! It felt real, but, clearly, situations such as this one were out of the realm of every day reality and more like a perverse episode straight from *The Twilight Zone*. She half expected to hear Rod Serling's voice echo throughout the cave she was being held a sexual hostage in at any given moment.

Slurp. Slurp. Slurp. Sluuuuuuuuurrrrrrrrrrp.

The more juice the manimal licked up, the bigger his penis grew. Beads of perspiration broke out on Dot's forehead at the realization of it. Was he going to penetrate her now? Oh sweet lord—nooooo! She didn't want that to happen. Not even in a dream.

Get up and run! Run, Dot! This isn't a dream!

Her mind was screaming that this odd situation was real. Her psyche gave her many reasons for believing as much, but it was the stark coldness of the cavern floor that underlined the horrifying fact this was really happening. Throughout her thirty-five years she'd experienced every sort of nightmare and pleasant imagining there was to be had in the world of slumber, but never once had she been able to feel such acute tactile sensations as bitter coldness.

It was real. She didn't know the how. She didn't comprehend the why. She had no idea where she was. But this was real.

Oh God.

Dot jarred herself upright into a sitting position, her eyes wide and her heart racing. Within the blink of an eye, the other four males were growling and attacking her, bodily forcing her to her back. One of the man-beasts sat behind her and stretched her arms out high above her head so that her breasts were thrust upward, a sexual offering to the others. Her pink nipples stabbed up into the air from a combination of cold and the orgasm she'd been awoken to.

"Stop it!" she screamed, hysteria rising. She struggled with everything she had in her, all to no avail. "Please—please let me go!"

A set of male lips found one erect nipple. His tongue snaked out, latched around it, and drew it in to the heat of his mouth. She whimpered. A second male mouth found her other nipple, again, making her whimper. By the time a third tongue touched her, the skinny, silky muscle invading her anus, she cried out, half moaning and half whining. God help her, she didn't know if the sound was from fright, arousal, or both.

The fifth male—the alpha male of this horde of creatures—stared at her splayed open pussy. He practically salivated as he watched it puff up and glisten. But he did nothing. Just sat there and stared at it, his fathomless black eyes in an almost trance-like state.

Dot groaned as the tongue in her anus fully penetrated her. It slid back and forth as if fucking her, slowly and with a sensuousness that was at odds with the force of the situation. She'd never felt anything like it before. She was frightened beyond comprehension, yet couldn't keep from moaning any sooner than she could keep from breathing.

The mouths at her breasts suckled her erect nipples harder. She gasped, her back involuntarily arching. That only served to thrust her breasts up like an offering, giving the creatures better access to her stiff nipples. They suckled them like lollipops, never tiring, each lick seemingly better to them than the last. The tongue in her anus kept up its slow, steady rhythm, driving her insane with a bizarre combination of terror and desire.

"Oh God," Dot breathed out. "Please...stop...stop...stop."

Her voice trailed off, fading more with each spoken word. Her entire body felt like it was on fire, being consumed by erotic, if perverse, flames. The creatures kept up their sucking, licking, and stroking. The smallest of the men-beasts continued to hold her hands high above her head so she couldn't move. All she could do was lie there and take it, her body being worked into a tight pitch of sensual nerve endings and sensations.

Her heart slammed against her chest. Her ragged breaths turned into steady moans. She tried to twist and turn, to escape the erotic ache being forced upon her, but the more she struggled the more intense the sexual longing became. The creatures sucked harder.

And harder. And harder.

The alpha male went in for the kill.

On a low growl, the leader of the creatures buried his head between Dot's thighs. She shouted out a warbled cry as his long, silky tongue stroked her clit. She screamed when his mouth latched around the sensitive piece of flesh and suckled it hard. He showed her no mercy, knowing as he had to that she was close to coming. He slurped her clit into his mouth over and over, again and again. Faster and faster and—

Dot burst into a million proverbial pieces, a violent orgasm ripping from her belly. *"Oh God,"* she gasped, blood rushing to her face, nipples, and cunt. Her nipples poked up so high it was at once pleasurable and painful. Her breathing was so ragged she feared fainting again. *"Oh God."*

Then, just like before, all five of the creatures scampered between her legs to lap at the flow of her juices with their long, skinny tongues. And, again just like before, the warning growl of the alpha male scared the others off.

The alpha male dined on her—literally—alone. He lapped up every bit of juice there was to extract from Dot, milking her like the teat of a damn cow. His cock grew in size and fierceness with each and every drop he took from her. She worried once again if now was when it—the thing—meant to rape her.

It didn't.

The sexual process repeated itself. Again. And again. And again. Early morning darkness became twilight and twilight became sunrise.

By the time Dot reached brutal orgasm number five, she had no juice left in her to give. The creatures must have realized as much for just that quickly they withdrew and she was forgotten.

Feeling weak and depleted, Dot sat up, open-jawed, as she warily watched the pack of beast-men scurry out of the cave they'd drug her into. Just like that. Weird. They'd made her come five times and then they left. *They are men all right!* There was no other word for the incredulousness of the situation other than weird.

She must have sat there a solid five minutes trying to make heads or tails of what had just transpired—and why. No answers were coming.

Snapping out of the daze that had engulfed her, Dot blinked and, feeling weak-kneed, dragged herself up to her feet. Her clothes had been torn to shreds. Without five warm hands, bodies, and tongues keeping her body temperature up, the bitter coldness of the environment began seeping into her bones.

She was drained of energy, but she recognized that she needed to get out of the cave and into her car—and as far away from this weird place as possible. A gnawing, gut-wrenching feeling inside told her escape from this bizarre world wouldn't be so easy as that, but there had to be a way. She just needed to find it.

Where there is an in, she mentally reminded herself as she walked on wobbly legs toward the cavern entrance, there is also an out. Figuring out where she was and how she'd gotten here wasn't nearly as important as finding that out.

Naked and shivering, Dot slowly, cautiously, crept out of the concealment of the cave. Her eyes nervously darted back and forth as she looked for her car.

Chapter Four

There it was. The sedan.

Shaky legs or no shaky legs, Dot dashed from the semi-protection the cave offered and toward her car as fast as her feet would carry her. Her large breasts bobbed up and down so fast that it hurt, but she didn't care. She just wanted to get inside her car.

And as far away from this horrible place as possible.

"Almost there," she panted, running faster. She could hear the crunch of freshly fallen snow under her feet but paid it no attention. She held her arms against her chest to keep her breasts from bobbing every which way. "Keep moving."

It was bitterly cold, snow and ice surrounding her on all sides. Her feet were so chilled they were numb, her skin a shield of goosebumps. She ignored everything, concentrated only on getting to her sedan.

By the time Dot reached the car, her breathing was so heavy and her teeth chattering so badly that she felt certain she was going to die. She whimpered when she came face to face with the non-existent driver's side door, only then recalling that it had been torn off the hinges by one of those creatures.

And just what were those creatures? she asked herself for what felt like the hundredth time as she got in the car, revved up the engine, and turned the heater to full blast. She'd never encountered anything like them, had never even heard any bigfoot-esque urban legends regarding menu-beasts that resembled those ones. Men-beasts who dined on a woman's juices no less! It was totally perverse. It reminded her of a sci-fi series she'd once read that had been penned by a weird (but highly creative) author of erotic romances. The only difference between that series and this reality in so far as she could tell was there would be no hero to save the day. Getting out of this situation was completely up to Dot.

The blast from the heater felt so good that she closed her eyes for a protracted moment and breathed in deeply. The icy chill creeping in from the missing driver's side door was the only negative that kept the experience from being the nirvana that it should have been.

Thinking quickly, Dot turned off the engine, jumped out of the car and ran around to the trunk. She popped it open, pulled out a few empty garbage bags she'd thankfully been too lazy to throw out, grabbed a reel of duct tape, slammed the trunk shut, and dashed back to the inside of the sedan. After re-revving the engine, she set to work at making a mock door that would, while not perfect, at least keep most of the bone-chilling cold outside where it belonged.

It worked. Within moments, Dot was warm, toasty, and sighing contentedly. She let herself bask in the glorious heat for a long moment before forcing herself to the task at hand — getting the hell out of dodge.

What a night! What a night! What a night!

Had she been out of harm's way at home, she would have had to dramatically recap the events she'd endured within the last several hours in order to brood over them. (She was good like that.) The martyr routine would, unfortunately, have to wait for later. Until she actually *found* home and could do said brooding safely. She was naked and shell-shocked — she wanted the hell out of here.

Putting the car into driving mode, Dot lightly pressed the gas pedal with her foot and drove back toward the thick forest of icy trees that had once engulfed her. It was the only rational direction she could think to take. Somewhere in those trees lay the key to Alice getting out of the rabbit hole and back to a reality where the rules, if imperfect, at least made some modicum of sense.

"Please, God," Dot muttered to herself, "let me find home." Suddenly smog, clogged California traffic, and actors-turned-governors didn't seem like such a bad thing. She'd take them, hands down, over men with tails and pupil-less black eyes any day of the week. "I promise to go to mass again," she said tragically, her voice squeaky. "And I'll quit sending Henry hate SPAM to his email address." (Maybe.) "And I'll—"

Her bartering with God came to a halt. Dot slammed on the brakes. She shook her head, unable to believe what she was seeing.

Those…things. They were just off to the left. And they had another female cornered. *Oh no!*

Dot didn't know what to do or how to help the other woman. Those creatures were super fast and unbelievably strong. The last run-in with them had resulted in her driver's side door being ripped off its hinges! What could she, naked and unarmed, possibly do to help? But how could she leave another female to the same fate? What kind of a person would that make her?

Nostrils flaring, Dot's eyes narrowed into wicked brown slits as she spun the steering wheel left, floored the gas pedal and drove top-speed toward the pack of men-beasts. Adrenaline surged through her blood. She gripped the steering wheel tightly. She felt like G.I. Jane on a mission.

Men suck! All of them! Even the ones with tails!

Feeling instant camaraderie with the pack's next victim, Dot flew toward the creatures like a NASCAR superstar. She would save this fellow female come hell or high water.

The closer she got, the more she could see of what the beasts were doing to their newest captive. Oh sweet lord…the man-beasts weren't just orally stimulating this poor woman to milk her for her juices. The leader of the pack was penetrating her—raping her! The other four held the growling, shrieking, mad-as-all-hell female down while the alpha male got his rocks off. The alpha male held up his victim's tail and penetrated her from behind, nipping at her neck and growling her into submission and…

Dot slammed on the brakes. Her jaw dropped open. The realization jarred her as much as the quick stop did:

The female had a tail, too.

Dot sat there in her sedan and stared, morbid curiosity overwhelming her, the scientific wheels in her mind spinning. Those manimals had captured Dot. The alpha male, and only the alpha male, had drank from her juices. The more he drank, the more swollen his cock had become. And then the beasts had left. And now the alpha male was — was he trying to impregnate this female of his species?

What a night! What a night! What a night!

"Oh how gross," Dot murmured. *Could this be how they mate?* "I can't believe I'm seeing this." Or that her orgasms had somehow helped this disgusting mating process along.

She slapped a palm to her forehead and whimpered. This was just too much.

Preparing to put the sedan in reverse and find her way out of this nightmare, a deafening roar pierced the icy valley, echoing throughout the mountains. The sound was so low and lethal that it sent a chill coursing down Dot's spine. It must have scared off the pack of things as well, for a mere second after the alpha male spurted inside the female of his species, all six of the creatures scampered off into the thick of the forest.

Dot might not be an aficionado at anything save inventing sex toys, but she knew when to take a cue. Whatever had issued that horrific growling sound was deadly — and no doubt a lot bigger than those already brawny creatures that had previously kidnapped her and held her hostage until they'd gotten what they wanted from her. Otherwise, they wouldn't have scampered off the way they did.

Alice, it's time to find your way out of the rabbit hole…

Putting the car in reverse, Dot swung the sedan around as fast as it could move, switched the gear to Drive, and took off like a bat out of hell. She drove toward the forest as if her life depended on it. She realized with dawning terror that it just might.

Another roar. Impossibly louder this time. He/It was getting closer.

Dot's heart slammed against her chest like a bucket of stones. She didn't know how, didn't understand why, but she knew beyond a shadow of doubt that this newer, deadlier threat was chasing her in particular. And only her.

"This is not happening!"

Another blood-curdling roar. And then he was there.

Dot's eyes widened in terror as she saw a huge, silver, winged creature descend from the heavens like an avenging angel—or demon. The closer he got, the larger he looked. "Holy shit!"

She floored the gas pedal, screaming as the realization she was being hunted by a gargoyle firmly took root...and sent a wave of terror through her that made the fright she'd experienced from the men-beasts with tails pale in comparison. This new threat was at least twice the size of the alpha male in that last pack in terms of musculature—and no doubt a thousand times more deadly.

And he—it—wanted *her*.

Vaidd could smell her fear, could sense her panic and desire to be as far away from him as 'twas possible. Verily, he wished it could be otherwise, yet he would claim her no matter what she felt, or didn't feel, for him.

The instinctual need to impregnate his female nigh unto consumed him. The scent of her sweet, sticky cunt beckoned to him, made his already erect shaft grow harder. He had to have her the soonest.

She would grow to love him. Six lifetimes they would spend together. That she feared and loathed him in this brief moment mattered naught. All that was of consequence to Vaidd was claiming what was rightfully his. And this primitive female *was* his.

The loneliness. The desolate ache that had consumed him from having spent so many Yessat Years without her. No laughter. Little joy. Grim countenance. Dead heart.

That was about to change.

Swooping down toward the odd moving mechanism his *vorah* was trying to escape from him in, Vaidd hissed in a way in which females of his species would immediately recognize meant, "you better come to me, wench, or else". His woman paid his warning growl no heed. He would have been amused were he not so coldly intent on catching her, so desperate to claim her.

Khan-Gori m'alana fey, zya. I will not harm you, little one.

He sent out the mental call, realizing she could not understand his language, but hoping she sensed the gentleness behind the message. He sent out the wave again in the tongue of his pack. *Khan-Gori m'alana fey, zya.* Mayhap her heart would understand even if her ears did not.

But still she sought to escape him. She continued moving in the metal box, shrieking words he did not understand as she attempted to thwart capture.

On a primal, territorial, "you better obey me *now*" roar rather than a warning hiss, Vaidd plunged down from the sky and landed upon the front of the metal box. His pupils narrowed and his crimson eyes flared as he bared his fangs at his *vorah*. She screamed from behind an odd, flimsy sort of window, her beautiful eyes wide with fear of him.

The metal box came to a smoking, grinding stop under Vaidd's unforgiving weight. The ensuing screams that gurgled up from his primitive woman's throat nigh unto gave his head the ache. Verily, he decided, 'twas high-pitched enough to make a lesser Barbarian wince.

Vaidd winced.

Grunting, he determined 'twas time to claim what was his, and hopefully call a halt to the near-deafening squeals. His ears were far too sensitive, his hearing too acute, for wails such as those. Growling low in his throat, he used a razor sharp fingernail to cut through the top of the metal box, and then with the mightiness of his biceps, picked it up and threw it aside.

The shrieking grew worse as his naked *vorah* tried to scoot away. He felt nigh unto dizzy from the hellish sound of it. Or mayhap that's just what he told himself so as not to feel the lovesick dunce. In truth, being this close to her, smelling the scent of his one, was so heady as to be drugging. She was trapped. She was perfect.

And she was all his.

Dot didn't know whether to faint, cry, scream, or do a combination of all three. She decided to keep screaming as she quickly glanced around for a weapon—any weapon.

Immediately ascertaining that she had nothing to protect herself with, save a few sex toys still lying in the passenger seat, she made do. Picking up "Freddy-The-Fish" and wielding him at the eight-foot gargoyle like a talisman, she blindly threw the cunnilingus toy at the giant. It struck home. Kinda.

Breathing heavily, Dot's shrieking calmed as she watched Freddy's mouth latch onto the gargoyle's cock and start sucking. The giant stilled, his red eyes slowly rolling to the back of his head.

He liked it! The inventor in Dot couldn't help but to see dollar signs light up in her eyes. Doh! She should have marketed a "Fredrika-The-Fish" toward male clients. (She made a mental note to get started on that project as soon as she escaped.)

Deciding there was no better time to try and flee into the forest than when the towering hulk was distracted, Dot subtly began to slide toward what was once a driver's side door. Realizing the garbage bags had gone the way of the car's hood, she knew her best chance at getting away was now.

The adrenaline began to pump faster, surging through her. She was naked—how could she survive in the freezing cold temperature without clothes? It didn't matter. She'd die here anyway. The fangs, claws, and talons the gargoyle was sporting told her that he probably wasn't a vegetarian.

Unfortunately, as soon as Dot began creeping towards the way out, the giant became aware of her presence again. And oh dear did he look angry. Not good.

Tearing Freddy's mouth off from around his cock with a popping sound, the huge male flung the toy away from him and growled with such loud intensity that Dot had to cover her ears. *What do I do now? God…please help me!*

More terrified than ever before, she snatched up "Diesel Dirk", stood up on the seat, and wielded the 10-inch vibrating cock like a baseball bat. "Come on!" she spat. Jaw clenching, she decided she wouldn't become sushi without a fight. "You want some of me?" she challenged. "Let's go!"

Later she would question her sanity. For now, feigning a lack of fear was all she could think to do.

Dot could have sworn she heard the gargoyle sigh. She supposed she couldn't blame him. She probably looked as formidable as a plump, juicy fish did to a hungry bear. All protein, no fear.

Her adrenaline running high, Dot aimed the baseball bat— Dirk—at the giant's torso and swung with all of her might. In a lightning-fast motion, the gargoyle snatched Dirk out of her grasp. She stilled. He licked his fangs.

Oh fuck.

"I-I really don't taste that good," Dot squeaked, shaking like a leaf in a hurricane. She tried to think of a tastier alternative than her flesh—one that might appease the giant and his no doubt voracious appetite. Thinking quickly, she fell back into the seat and popped open the glove compartment. *Snack cakes? That's it? Arrrrrg!* It would have to do.

"Here boy," she said calmly, if a bit unsteadily. Dot held up the solitary package of stale snack cakes she had left in the sedan and dangled them in front of him with a weak smile. She couldn't think of anything else to do! She'd heard of things like feeding sugar cubes to horses and fish to dolphins in order to endear one's self to the animals in question, but the subject of gargoyle snacks had never come up in parochial school. "These are r-really good," she shakily encouraged him. "T-Try one."

Her eyes round, Dot hastily licked her dry lips as she watched the giant pluck the snack cake from her grasp with a gentleness she had not been anticipating. A silver hand with five razor-sharp black claws took the gift, held it to his nose and sniffed, and then proceeded to swallow it whole, wrapper and all. The scene brought to mind a killer shark being fed a cracker—definitely not filling enough to appease.

Okay, smart one, now what?

Up until now, Dot's gaze had skittishly avoided the giant's. Shy to her grave, she supposed. But something she couldn't explain, some force beyond her understanding, told her to look him in the eyes. She did. She hesitated for a brief moment, but she did.

Crimson red eyes clashed with frightened doe-shaped brown ones. An instant calm settled over her. Words filled her mind—foreign words she didn't understand. The longer she stared at the gargoyle, the further her consciousness drifted. Away and away, a feather in a gentle wind...

Dot closed her eyes for a brief moment, a trance-like state enveloping her, engulfing every fiber of her being. When next she flicked her eyes open, she saw the giant reaching toward her, beckoning her to go to him. It felt like it was happening to somebody else.

One second she was seated in the sedan. The next she was in his leathery embrace, her arms around his neck. She swallowed a bit heavily as her gaze once again found his. She blinked several times in rapid succession, shaking the trance-like, surreal feeling off.

Dot was given no time to rethink the fact that she'd just gone into the gargoyle's arms willingly. A rumbled growl and a push up from two powerful thighs later, the giant and his captive shot up into the air and took flight, leaving all hopes of escape for Dot far behind.

Suddenly she wished she'd kept more snack cakes in the car.

Chapter Five

Wings fiercely swooping up and down, his *vorah* securely in his arms, Vaidd flew at top speed back toward the hunting grounds of the Zyon pack. The need to claim her, to mark her as his possession, was nigh unto overwhelming. His cock was stiff with aching need to sink deep inside of her sticky, tight flesh. Yet Vaidd had captured his wench in enemy territory. The instinct to protect what was his pounded inside of him as ruthlessly as the instinct to become one with her —

Verily, she was his key. His key to sanity. His only hope at escaping from the dark void within. Without her he would choose death. There would be no reason to evolve a second time when the next *gorak* came for there was but *one*.

Vaidd could sense his *vorah's* distress. He knew that she didn't understand what was happening, where they were going, or what fate would befall her. Until he could drink of her blood, and she of his, there would be no answers forthcoming for her. Verily, he had no means until the mating to communicate with her in a tongue she could comprehend.

She wasn't the only confused one for Vaidd found himself questioning just how it 'twas a primitive had found her way to Khan-Gor. Very few within his own dimension of space and time even realized that the ice-planet existed. 'Twas believed, as the elders of the packs had wanted outsiders to believe, that Khan-Gor was naught but a legend. And so it had been for millions of Yessat Years.

Vaidd found himself not caring about the how and the why. Mayhap not even his Bloodmate understood how she had come to be here. And truly, it mattered not. She was here. 'Twas all that he had a care for.

In a few minutes more, Vaidd Zyon would be firmly within the stronghold of his pack. And then, at long last, he could claim his woman for all eternity.

* * * * *

Dot held onto the giant's neck for dear life. His massive arms were securely around her middle, but she was taking no chances. Plus his leathery skin kept her naked body feeling toasty warm.

If there had been any lingering doubts but that Dot had somehow, ludicrous and insane as it sounded, been transported into another world, they were laid to rest in mid-air. This icy cold place was unlike anything she'd ever seen before.

The trees below, when not coated in ice, were either purple or a blackish-blue—colors rarely seen in any vegetation back on earth except for maybe flowers and the occasional eggplant. Four suns hung in the skies—they were far away—so far away that the heat they radiated couldn't penetrate the bitter coldness of the atmosphere—but they were there. Foreign, bizarre birds flew by, weird looking animals with multiple heads stampeded below…

No. Dot was most definitely not on earth.

She didn't know where they were, where they were going or, most importantly, what would happen to her once they got there. The endless scenarios swimming through her mind ranged from being dinner to becoming a gargoyle's sex slave. She didn't know which possibility was worse.

If her captor killed her quickly and waited to make a meal of her post-mortem, well, she didn't want to die but at least that was a merciful death. Now if he preferred his food fresh and still alive while eating…

She whimpered. *Sweet lord, please don't let that happen!*

Unfortunately, becoming the gargoyle's sex slave didn't seem any more appealing than being human sushi. Both ways lay torture. She could feel his stiff cock underneath her naked bottom—she was using it as a seat for goodness sake!—and lordy, lordy was his manhood huge. He made her well-endowed sex toys look like prepubescent boys. For the first time in four years, Dot grimly understood just why Henry had fainted when she'd held up Dirk. She felt a bit on the dizzy, swooning side herself. Fate, it seemed, had a perverse sense of humor.

And by the way, God, when I was fantasizing all those years about being swept off my feet by an extremely tall, muscular, hunky, alpha male kind of guy...this was NOT what I had in mind!

Apparently she should have been more specific in her platitudes to the higher power, she thought tragically. But it was too late, and she knew it.

They began to descend. Dot's gaze immediately honed in on the cave they were heading toward. She shivered, her eyes widening, as she wondered what exactly would happen to her in this cave. The memory of what had transpired in the last one was still fresh in her mind. It had only ended, after all, but a few hours ago.

Dot had no notion as to what vile plans the gargoyle had in mind for her, but one certainty was crystal clear: he had no intention of releasing her. It didn't take an educated guess to figure that much out. Not with the way he was holding onto her as if he might never get a hold of a plumper, better meal.

With a heavy heart and stoic resolution, she realized that the giant wouldn't let her escape him alive—

Ever.

* * * * *

At long last they reached the Zyon hunting grounds. Vaidd realized that a celebratory feast for his return from *gorak* most likely lay in waiting within the sanctum—the large gathering place deep within the village's innermost cavern where all ceremonial and religious gatherings of the pack occurred. His fellow Barbarians would be expecting his return from *gorak*. What they would not be anticipating, however, was Vaidd's homecoming from the sleep of the dead with his Bloodmate in tow.

That his woman happened to be a primitive...

Verily, 'twould be the talk of all Khan-Gor. There was but one other female primitive—Nancy—who dwelled within the whole of the ice-planet, and forever was her Bloodmate keeping her close to his side. Vorik took no chances that another male might wish to steal her for *vorah* theft did happen every now and again. 'Twas rare, for a true mating was what Barbarians coveted, but the depths a Khan-Gori would sink to when nearing the end of another lifetime and still without a Bloodmate...

Like Vorik, Vaidd would take no chances with his wench either. He had waited a full lifetime to find her—that he was possessive of her was an understatement for a certainty.

On a roar his people would understand announced his return from the sleep of the dead, Vaidd landed on two feet at the mouth of Zyon Rock—the entrance to the pack's village. He could feel his Bloodmate tense up, understood that she knew not what was to transpire.

They needed to mate. Their blood needed to mingle. Until it did, she would have no comprehension of his words, his pack's language. And he would have no understanding of anything she spoke to him either. But once their blood did mingle, they would be able to communicate freely. 'Twas the way of the all-knowing gods.

Setting his Bloodmate down on two shaky feet, he stood her before him. The entryway at Zyon Rock was a wee bit cold to her delicate humanoid form, yet bearable.

His cock swelled just staring at her. She was beautiful, so very perfect in every way. Long waves of hair in a hue of light brown he'd never before seen, two gorgeous eyes a deeper, richer color of the same shade. Full breasts. Long legs. Plump in all the right places.

Lifting a hand toward her in a non-threatening, slow manner, Vaidd palmed her chin and patiently waited for her to meet his gaze. To her credit, she did—no hypnotism necessary. She was nervous, he knew, but she'd still looked up at him.

Vaidd slowly threaded his lethal black fingernails through the soft waves of her hair. He didn't smile, but his emotions were there in his eyes.

I've waited so long to find you, little one. Mayhap you fear me now, but soon you will understand that no harm shall ever come to you. Verily, you are the only one in existence who need not fear me. I will protect you with my own life.

The mental call was in his own tongue, so Vaidd realized she had no comprehension of his words. Yet he hoped her heart understood.

As his *vorah* stood there and watched, Vaidd shape-shifted from his *kor-tar* form and back to his humanoid one. His face hard and stoic, he watched his Bloodmate gasp and back away from him.

She stood there for a long while, her jaw agape, as if trying to work things out in her mind. He shape-shifted back into his *kor-tar* form, then again to his humanoid one—this time donning the clothing of his clan, that she might know her eyes were not deceiving her.

Apparently males of her species were not able to take on other forms. 'Twas the only explanation Vaidd could fathom for a moment later his wench's gorgeous eyes rolled to the back of her head…and she fainted.

Dot blinked several times in rapid succession, unable to believe what she was seeing. One second there was a gargoyle there and then the next—holy shit!—there was a man standing before her. A very, very capital B-I-G for BIG, naked man. He must have stood seven and a half to eight feet tall. His hair was a light brown with golden streaks, his eyes like molten silver. His body was heavily muscled, a jagged scar zigzagging down the right side of his torso. His cock was just as ferociously swollen now as it had been while in gargoyle mode.

No way.

She gasped, backing away. There was *no way* that...

He shifted again—back to the gargoyle. And then again—back to the man.

Now he was clothed. Sorta. His chest was bare, but he wore a black and red kilt-like skirt that stopped mid-thigh...huge, massively sculpted thighs! The dark leather boots he was sporting ended just below the knee.

Dot began feeling dizzy. Until last night she'd never fainted before in her life. Now she wondered if it was to become an average, daily event for her.

Breathe, Dot, breathe. Slow, deep breaths. Slower. Deeper. Arrrrrrrrg!

Unfortunately, nothing short of a tranquilizer was likely to make her breasts stop heaving up and down. This was just too much to take in. This man, this-this...*thing*...spent part of his time looking like a wicked nightmare straight out of a B-rated horror movie and the other part of it looking like a human—an incredibly gigantic human but still a human.

And she was standing in front of him naked no less! Somehow, when he'd been a gargoyle, her state of undress hadn't much mattered; it had been like standing in the nude in front of a creature at the zoo. Not a big deal, other than the fact she was likely to become his dinner. But now her nudity bothered her—a lot.

She was a poster girl candidate for the all-American, Catholic, sexually frustrated spinster for the love of God! She invented large, vibrating penises for her pleasure because she was too shy to meet the real deal. Talking to men she didn't know could welt up her entire body with a case of nervous hives. Standing in front of one naked was not precisely a walk in the park.

Oh dear God in heaven, why hast thou forsaken me?

A prayer straight from the drama queen bible, perhaps, but Dot felt as though she had that moment of martyrdom coming to her and then some. Her first instinct was to cover up her various intimate parts with her hands as best as she could manage. She never got that far. The entire situation frayed her nerves like violin strings that had been strung so tightly they snapped at the first pluck.

Her jaw agape while she stared at the large male as though he had two heads — and for all intent and purposes he did! — Dot's brown eyes slowly rolled to the rear of her head. Stiff as a board, she plunged straight backwards.

And, yea, though I walk through the valley of the shadow of death…oh…never mind!

Arrrrrrg!

Chapter Six

Vaidd's nostrils flared as he roared in his throat, customarily acknowledging his pack members' boisterous clapping, hissing, and growling. Some shifted into their *kor-tar* form, some merely sprouted fangs and roared back at him.

His sire's eyes widened. As Vaidd strode into the sanctum, the sight of his eldest son's Bloodmate asleep in his arms was more of a triumph to him and the rest of the pack than even was Vaidd's return from *gorak*.

Their line, unlike that of so many other Barbarian packs, would go on.

Verily, Vaidd's mother had entered her fifth lifetime and his sire the seventh. The pack's matriarch was still within childbearing years, though the patriarch was not. Male Khan-Gori became sterile once they left their sixth lifetime. 'Twas the way of the gods. Why, none knew.

Vaidd's mother had delivered nigh unto two hundred pups in her prime, only three of which were female. Obviously Vaidd's three sisters could not mate within their own pack— such caused madness amongst the offspring. Never had Vaidd heard tell of a Barbarian finding his *vorah* in a sister! Leastways, Nitara, Vala, and Saris had yet to find their true Bloodmates. Even when and if they did, 'twould be another pack's line that his sisters furthered, not his own. Unless, of course, their mates were not of Khan-Gor.

"I have returned from the sleep of the dead," Vaidd rumbled out. His silver eyes were heated, his expression cold and merciless. "With my *vorah*," he growled. Using both hands, he held her naked, unconscious body up like a trophy. He waited for the congratulatory noise to dim before continuing.

"As the heir to our clan," he shouted, that all his brothers gathered in the sanctum might hear his voice echoing off the stony, cavern walls, "I have upheld ceremony and waited to join with my Bloodmate until I brought her back to our lair."

His sire nodded his respect of the decision. His brothers hissed theirs. 'Twas not easy for a predator to stay away from the cunt of his mate. The instinctual need to impregnate her had nigh unto overwhelmed Vaidd more than once. The scent of it alone was intoxicating. Holding her naked in his arms had all but driven him mad.

Mayhap 'twas not an accident of nature that Khan-Gori females were so few in number. The average *vorah* could bear up to ten litters throughout her lifetimes. Some, like his mother, bore more, and some less. Should more females come to be, all of them bearing litter after litter of hungry pups, 'twould take an ugly toll on the food chain for a certainty.

And so it was that the mated brother of the pack became the Alpha upon the extinction of their sire's seventh lifetime — even if that brother was not the first-born. Did two brothers within a pack both find their mates — a rarity — the Alpha position was bequeathed to the eldest. Did no brothers of a pack find a mate, again, the Alpha position fell to the eldest. Such was why Vaidd had been named his sire's heir apparent prior to this claiming. When a Barbarian reached his seventh lifetime and none of his sons had mated, 'twas when he formally named his eldest the assumed heir.

Vaidd felt fiercely proud at the offering he was bestowing unto his sire. His father would not join the gods in the Underworld thinking that surely his line was to die off. The she-god of mating had smiled down upon Vaidd. The Zyon bloodline would continue.

Vaidd's sire, Zolak, stood up. His voice was booming, his stance proud. "Let us welcome home your brother — my rightful heir!" he announced. "And let us rejoice at the claiming of his Bloodmate!"

Loud shouts, hisses, and roars filled the sanctum, emotion echoing off the stone walls. Some of the feelings were elation, a triumph that their line would go on. Some of the feelings were akin to despair, for all of the brothers realized 'twas rare for more than one male of the same pack to find a Bloodmate.

Vaidd's hard gaze softened when it landed upon his sister, Nitara. She was so overcome with relief and happiness at Vaidd's good fortune that her eyes had welled up with tears. Nitara and Vaidd had been born of the same litter—the first litter. 'Twas therefore no surprise that their bond had always been a close one.

"Let the claiming begin!" Zolak bellowed, diverting Vaidd's attention back to his sire.

Vaidd cradled his Bloodmate's wee, warm, limp body close to his heart. His fangs couldn't help but to burst out from his gums, so aroused he was. The smell of her skin, the scent of her pussy, urged the animal in him on.

At long last, it was time to claim what was his.

* * * * *

Dot awoke to the sight of hungry gargoyles surrounding her everywhere. She had been strewn out naked on a table, laid in the middle of what looked to be a platter. She knew this was it—sushi city. The only things missing from the scene were an apple in her mouth and various sauces for the wicked beasts to dip her flesh in for their dining pleasure. Instead of chicken nuggets, they'd be getting raw Dot nuggets.

So this is what will become of me? I gave you my last snack cake, you bastard. So much for generosity!

Dot's nostrils flared at the bastard in question. All gargoyles looked alike, but for reasons unknown she could pick her captor out of a line-up that featured one thousand of the things. "I will haunt you from my grave," she ardently vowed. "And I hope I taste like shit!"

One of the gargoyles — not her captor — began speaking. He used words Dot could not understand. All of the gargoyles then joined hands in a circle around her, closed their eyes, and bowed their heads.

Good grief. They had formed a prayer circle around her, no doubt thanking whatever god they worshipped for the bounty they were about to receive! Suddenly she understood what it felt like to be the turkey on Thanksgiving Day.

At least I had enough heart to buy a turkey that was already dead. I hope I give all of you food poisoning and really super bad indigestion!

She hoped they farted her for weeks — a reminder not to go snatch innocent women from their vehicles ever again. And if there was any justice whatsoever in this horrible world of theirs, they'd be belching up Dot nuggets until they took their last breaths.

Dot's mind began to splinter. She felt one small inch away from insanity. This was just too much. The men-beasts with tails had been bad enough. Now she was being prayed over by a pack of gargoyles before they sat down to dine on Dot a l'orange.

She began to scream, a deafening, shrill cry that resonated throughout the stone chamber she'd awoken in and gained everyone's undivided attention. She screamed louder and impossibly more high-pitched.

Their chanting immediately stopped. They began to hiss, all of them except her captor covering their ears. But even he looked ready to pass out.

She'd found a weapon! Oh yes! Oh yes! She just hoped her lungs and vocal chords would comply long enough to get the hell out of here.

Bolting up from her back and onto her feet, Dot stopped screaming and prepared to jump off the table. As soon as her shrieking ceased, the gargoyles all grabbed for her. She screamed again, a piercing sound that made even her wince, as she stood on the platter in a karate "come-get-me-fucker" position. She moved her arms back and forth like an expert in the martial arts anticipating the enemy's next move.

They recovered their ears. She kept up the shrill noise as she jumped off the platter and headed toward the nearest exit.

Where is the way out? I don't need any more complications, God. My lungs are about to implode!

"By the tit of the she-god," one of Vaidd's brothers whimpered, "shut thy wench up!"

"She means to flee from us!" his sire yelled as he kept his sensitive ears covered up. He nodded toward where Vaidd's shrieking Bloodmate was running in circles, desperately trying to find a way out.

Vaidd felt nigh close to swooning from the horrid, deafening noise his *vorah* was making, yet he stumbled as best he could toward her. That, unfortunately, only made her more frantic. Her large, dark eyes widened as she screamed impossibly louder.

'Twas like a kick in the man sac. Vaidd fell to his knees and gasped, trying to regain control of himself that he might regain control of the situation. 'Twas sorely apparent why primitive wenches were hard to tame—or at least one of the reasons why. Verily, they were possessed of wicked defenses. Vaidd grimly realized that his friend Vorik deserved a Khan-Gori medal of valor for the claiming of Nancy.

His eyes narrowing into merciless slits, he forced himself up from his knees and sprang toward his Bloodmate. Her screaming grew worse. But, thank the gods, through gritted teeth and a perspiring brow, he managed to catch her. And then he did something he knew every member of his pack would be forever grateful for—he slapped a palm over her mouth.

The shrieking ceased. All Khan-Gori present breathed a sigh of relief.

* * * * *

This time when they put her on the platter, they tied her down and placed some sort of adhesive that smelled like pinecones over her mouth. Naked, her arms had been hoisted above her head and her legs splayed wide open and secured down. Her ass was at the very end of the platter, almost suspended off the table itself.

As they formed their satanic prayer circle around her once again, Dot realized it was time to give up the ship. She was dead meat and there was no stopping it.

The gargoyles continued to chant, eyes closed, bald heads bowed, to their higher power. She simply couldn't believe this was happening. One minute she'd been heading toward a bachelorette party to sell her sex toys and the next she'd become the main entrée on a gargoyle menu.

Breathing in deeply through her nose, Dot found her courage. They had won, but she would go down with dignity, strength, and pride. (She'd always loved those movies where the fallen hero or heroine died like that.) Yes, she thought wistfully, her life would end on a note of bravery and fortitude. Dorothy Araiza—American heroine extraordinaire. If her people ever found this world and unearthed her skeletal remains, they would surely bury her with eloquent style. Not that it would do her much good because she'd be dead. But oh well, that wasn't the point.

The chanting came to an abrupt halt. The gargoyles lifted their heads and all eyes turned to Dot. Her heartbeat sped up and her gaze widened.

On the other hand, dying with dignity was highly overrated.

Dot began screaming from behind the adhesive, her hands and feet trying to break free from their confinements. She rattled at the ties that bound her, her body shaking and breasts jiggling, all to no avail.

The large, all-encompassing prayer circle broke off into several smaller ones. Ten of the creatures formed the innermost circle around her. Twenty or so creatures formed a circle around them, and so on.

The end was here. Tired and resigned, Dot gave up the good fight and quit squirming. She had raged, she had battled, and she had lost. All good soldiers knew when the hour of doom was upon them. Her last and final hope was that the creatures would show her mercy and knock her out before beginning their dirty deed. Hit her over the head with a hammer, decapitate her—whatever. She just didn't want to be awake for it.

The gargoyles shifted into human forms, making Dot go still. She had thought she'd dreamt that part about her captor— obviously not! She morbidly wondered just why they had bothered shifting into humanoid forms to begin with. One would think it would be easier to tear her apart from limb to limb with claws, talons, and fangs at the ready.

Her captor, the one who had somehow managed to mesmerize her into going willingly into his arms, stood naked and erect between her spread open thighs. Nine other males surrounded her, all of them clothed in that red and black kilt-like skirt with no shirt.

The compulsion to look her vanquisher in the eyes was an overwhelming one. Unlike the last time, Dot now realized it was a form of hypnotism. Knowing what it was, however, didn't make her any better able to resist this time than it had the last.

Her gaze found his. An instant calm stole over her. It felt just like a tranquilizer. When he removed the adhesive from over her mouth, she didn't scream. Instead, the feeling lingered. This time, for whatever reason, she seemed unable to snap out of it. "Han kana," she heard her subjugator murmur. She had no idea what it meant, but the dreamy state that enveloped her kept her from caring.

Two of the clothed males palmed either of Dot's breasts. She felt nothing but pleasure, unable to experience apprehension. They used both of their hands to massage her there, each of them attuned to a single breast. Another set of hands found her arms and massaged them. Another set her legs. Another set her belly. The only part of her that wasn't being intimately stroked was her vagina. Her captor took care of that.

He stroked her pussy softly, sensuously, as their gazes remained locked. He murmured words to her that she didn't comprehend, but that did a number on her hormones.

Dot's breasts were being kneaded in the same gentle, intoxicating manner. Her nipples were pulled at and played with like firm clay in a potter's hands — doing whatever those hands wanted to do with her to elicit the response they were going for. They got it.

She moaned softly, a knot of arousal forming in her belly as the gigantic males worked her body up into a fevered pitch. Her already stiff nipples jutted up further into the air, giving greedy mouths plenty to suck on. She closed her eyes as the feeling of teeth scraping her nipples and enveloping them into hot mouths overwhelmed her. They sucked on her nipples hard while her captor massaged her wet clit, causing her to shiver. Dot cried out, unable to keep herself from responding to the exquisite pleasure.

Something poked at her moist entrance, inducing her eyes to fly open. Him — the one who held the power to mesmerize her — he was trying to get his gigantic cock inside her. Apparently he was accustomed to bedding women with bigger holes, for perspiration dotted his hairline and his jaw was clenched at the effort.

It dawned on her that she should be feeling some sort of apprehension. His cock was HUGE — swollen, erect, and painfully big. She *should* have experienced fear, but she felt nothing but desire for him to be inside of her.

A soft, deep voice in her head kept telling her something, but what Dot had no idea. All she did know was the desire to be impregnated by her subjugator was an overwhelming one.

He rubbed her clit more briskly, making her head fall back on a groan. The mouths on her nipples sucked harder until she was gasping for air and moaning. Her breasts heaved up and down from under their mouths. Her hips instinctively reared up as far as they could given the restraints, pressing her wet flesh against her captor's swollen cock. He hissed as the head slipped in, her pussy enveloping it, holding it in with an unyielding grip.

The erotic body massage at so many hands and mouths was beyond anything. The mouths sucked her nipples harder. Her captor's thumb rubbed her clit faster. She could hear how wet she was, the sticky sound of her pussy being massaged reaching her ears.

"Oh God," Dot breathed out. *"I'm coming."*

She came loudly, violently, the intense coil in her belly springing loose. "Oh—*ooooooh!*" Blood rushed to her nipples and face, heating them. Her entire body convulsed, shaking. Unable to move, all she could do was lie there and groan like a dying animal.

He impaled her cunt in one smooth thrust, turning her groan into a whimper. She felt the pain, but couldn't experience the fear that should have accompanied it—the situation was akin to losing one's virginity while heavily intoxicated.

Fangs burst from his gums as he threw his head back on a roar of victory and possessiveness. The males surrounding them hissed and growled, all of their fangs baring, all of their silver eyes turning a haunting blood-red.

Dot couldn't look away from her captor's jugular vein to save herself. *What the hell is happening to me?* The compulsion to bite it, to taste his blood, was powerful. She couldn't blink, couldn't do anything besides lie there and want what she couldn't reach.

Her hands sprang free from the binds. Her legs were loosed next.

Their gazes clashed.

Still buried inside her to the hilt, her captor leaned over her comparatively tiny body and, looking to the side, bared his neck to her. Dot wouldn't understand the force that drew her to that gorgeous vein until much later, but she didn't care either. She just wanted it.

Wrapping her arms around his neck, she closed her eyes and sank her teeth into his jugular. He hissed and groaned in animalistic pleasure. Her human teeth were not able to tear through it, but were sufficiently strong to clamp it together — and pinch just hard enough to squeeze a few droplets of blood from his neck.

The sweet droplets of blood touched her tongue. Instinctively, she let her arms fall away from his neck. Arching her breasts up like an offering, she bared her neck to the half man half gargoyle.

He didn't go for her jugular, damn it! And though her human mind was wary in the deepest recesses of its consciousness, oh how her body wanted him to. Her womb repeatedly contracted at the mere thought of such. But, no, he wasn't ready. His deadly fangs grazed just above her heart instead, causing a few droplets of her blood to spill out. His tongue darted out, sensually lapping them up.

Dot screamed, the orgasm sudden and ruthless. He growled as she convulsed, her moans and blood an aphrodisiac.

He began to fuck her, pumping in and out of her cunt in long, territorial thrusts. She groaned, the scent of their combined arousal and the sound of her pussy suctioning in his cock on every outstroke a turn-on.

"Fuck her harder, Vaidd," one male purred.

"Your wife wants it harder," another one growled.

It occurred to Dot they were calling her his — her captor's — *wife!* It also dawned on her that she could understand what was being said. Words, once foreign, now infiltrated her entire being as native. She was given no time to figure out why.

"I am Vaidd," her vanquisher murmured, his teeth gritting from the tightness of her pussy. "And you," he said roughly, "are mine."

He fucked her harder, going primal on her, riding her body like he meant to brand every inch of her as his. Her tits jiggled with every thrust, moans pulled from her lips as though he was getting his wish. His eyes were fully crimson, fangs bared as he growled and roared out his pleasure.

"Oh God!" Dot screamed, her head falling back. Her eyes closed in an ecstasy she'd never before experienced. "*Yesssssss!*"

He pumped her cunt harder — faster — deeper — *more, more, more.*

In and out.

Over and over.

Again and again and again.

Sweat-slick skin slapped against sweat slick-skin. Her stiff nipples were further sensitized with every jiggle brought on by every of his thrusts. His jaw clenched as he fucked her, teeth gritting as he possessively sank his cock into her.

"I'm coming!" Dot groaned, her eyelids flying open. And this time she wanted that jugular when she came. She didn't know why she wanted it, only that her body was commanding her to bite it.

Baring her human teeth on a snarl to rival one of Vaidd's, Dot wrapped her arms around his neck and bit down. He roared out his pleasure, then, still fucking her, sank his fangs into her jugular as she clamped down onto his. Vaidd's blood hit her tongue, Dot's blood gushed onto his.

The mutually experienced orgasm was all-consuming, shattering, in its depths. Their mouths broke free in order to moan as both of them shook from the violence of it. Hot cum erupted, filling her insides. Blood trickled down her neck. They groaned and held each other tightly, riding out wave after delicious wave of erotic synergy.

When it was over, when both of their breathing had returned to a semi-normal state, Vaidd slowly withdrew his still-erect cock from Dot's flesh on a suctioning sound. Panting, he looked down into her eyes and laid her fully on her back as he released her from the spell that had enveloped her.

His eyes returned to silver with black pupils, flicking over her face, memorizing her features. "What is thy name, *zya*?" he purred.

Zya — little one.

"Dot," she whispered. Her brown eyes widened on a plethora of questions. But she decided to get out the most pressing one. "Does this mean you don't plan to eat me?" she squeaked. Dot couldn't imagine anyone making love to her like that, giving her the mother of all orgasms, only to turn her into gargoyle-chow. Not to mention the fact that the emotions radiating from him were almost overwhelming in their protective possessiveness. Still, she supposed anything could happen in a world like this.

Vaidd's gaze narrowed in incomprehension, then sparkled in mischievous understanding. "I'll eat you for a certainty, but not like that."

He didn't smile as the other members in the chamber began to boom with laughter, but his eyes were dancing and his purr was comforting.

"Well, that's a relief," she said dumbly. *I mean, really, what does one say in a situation like this!* She made to sit up. "Why can I understand what you're saying now, and vice versa, when I couldn't before? Why did you lay me on a platter if you didn't mean to eat me? And what in the world were those tailed things that dragged me into the cave? They had tails, okay! Oh and — "

He pressed two fingers gently against her lips. "In a sennight I shall answer all thy questions," he murmured.

A sennight! Thanks to all of the historical romance novels she'd read over the years, she realized what he meant. But, "Why a week?"

"Because."

She frowned. Wordy he was not. "Because why?"

He grunted. "Because 'tis time for my wee love to evolve." He motioned toward her legs.

Dot glanced down. She gasped in shock and more than a little fright. A sticky web-like substance was steadily encasing her feet…and crawling up higher to encase her everywhere. She screamed, beyond horrified, as she watched the web climb higher and higher and higher. Her heartbeat thumped wildly as it spread to her arms and her chest and—

"You shall be cocooned but a sennight, my love. Then you shall be of my species."

What a comfort!

"Why are you doing this to me?" Dot howled as the web began crawling up to encase her face. "A woman gives you snack cakes and you put her in a web!" The last part of her sentence was mumbled out as the web closed over her mouth.

Arrrrrg!

Chapter Seven
One week later

Vaidd paced as he waited and waited for his *vorah* to hatch. His cock was nigh unto stone it was so aching and swollen from this last sennight without her.

"Son," Zolak rumbled out, "take you a walk. Go hunt. Do something to distract thyself. Verily, you are driving the pack daft with the pacing. She will hatch when the metabolic changes within have fully occurred and not a moment before. This you know!"

He ran a hand over his jaw, sighing. His sire was correct and, as he'd said, he knew it. Glancing up to the *vorah-sac* suspended deep within the Zyon stronghold, he looked away and nodded his agreement. "Aye," he murmured. "I shall go for a walk."

There was more to his anxiety than a desire to mate, but Vaidd would not share feelings of the heart with his father. Namely, the scared, helpless manner in which Dot had last looked upon Vaidd before being cocooned nigh unto tore his heart clean out. He wanted her to hatch so she'd realize he would never hurt her, leave her, or in any way endanger her.

She was his—now and always. He could never do anything to harm her.

"Go, son," Zolak said softly, knowingly. "She will hatch before you know it."

He inclined his head and then walked away.

* * * * *

Air rushed into Dot's lungs, filling them. Her eyes flew open, fangs bursting from her gums. Claws shot out from her fingers and toes, spikes jutted up, forming a wristband of deadly pikes around either hand.

He was near. Her one.

The need to be impregnated overpowered her, beckoned to her, made every egg in her ovaries tingle. Dot shredded her cocoon faster than a great white shark could gulp a tuna and took to the air.

I'm flying! Oh dear lord I am flying!

The human memory cells in her brain were wary, but the primitive need to fill her womb with Vaidd's pups overrode everything. She was so horny she couldn't stand it, felt like she'd go insane if he didn't impale her and fuck her like the animal she now was.

She flew out of the cave and over a nearby stream. The scent of food momentarily distracted her. Swooping down, she snarled at her prey and, snatching it up from the icy water below, tore both heads off some sort of fish and gobbled it down.

Oh God, I've just eaten a two-headed fish! While. It. Was. Alive. Ohhhh noooooo!

A palm tragically lifting to her forehead, Dot's wings swooped with less and less vigor, until finally, she was on the ground. Glancing at her reflection in the stream, she felt the drama queen lance right through her.

I'm bald! I ate a two-headed fish while it was still alive and now I am bald!

Only whilst in kor-tari form, a deep voice answered in her mind. *And you are gorgeous in both forms to me.*

Dot's bald, silver head came up. Horniness returned as she saw Vaidd swooping down from the air. There went those damn eggs tingling again.

Well, she sniffed in her mind, *if I'm gorgeous to you then I suppose —*

He was on her in a heartbeat, covering her from behind, ready to fuck her. He growled her into submission, fangs bared as he took her down to her knees. She growled back—mostly just because she could and it felt kinda neat—then pressed her swollen pussy up into the air so he count mount her.

Vaidd sank into her flesh from behind, howling at the exquisite feel of her tight cunt enveloping and gripping his cock. He thrust into her to the hilt, then rode her hard, wasting no time in taking what he considered to be his.

"Yesss," Dot hissed. She glanced at him from over her shoulder and snarled. *"Fuck me harder."*

"Like this?" Vaidd growled, sinking deep into her cunt, over and over, again and again. He scratched at the sensitive skin of her hips with his claws, making her keen in pleasure. "Does my little one like it rough?"

Oh yes, Dot thought. She hadn't known she'd liked to be taken so animalistically prior to her evolution, but now there was no going back. And the hip thing…who knew?

"Scratch me harder! Fuck me harder! Get me pregnant!"

She didn't know what she wanted more—all of them. She was lost in a delirious haze of pleasure, wanting everything and anything her mate could give her.

Vaidd picked up the pace of their joining, hissing as he rooted inside her. He scratched her hips harder, fucked her harder—everything harder. He slammed into her cunt again and again, merciless in his domination.

And then he gave her his babies.

On a piercing roar, Vaidd lowered his head to his *vorah's* neck and sank his teeth deep inside the sweet, warm vein. She howled as she came, her entire body bucking and convulsing from the pleasure of it. Vaidd followed quickly behind, sinking into her cunt as fast and deep as he could, then spurting his seed deep into her pussy.

He wasn't done with his Bloodmate. Not even close.

By the time Vaidd picked up his wife and flew with her in his arms back to their lair, he had fucked her eight times. There was no question to Dot as to whether or not fertilization had occurred. She had known the second it had happened. A warm feeling, half primitive and half enlightened in nature, had engulfed her.

Life already grew in her belly.

* * * * *

They laid next to each other within the stronghold of the Zyon pack in humanoid form. Vaidd ran a callused hand through her chestnut-brown hair, his silver eyes all over her naked body. Seeing her gargoyle as a man didn't, surprisingly enough, make Dot go all shy on him this time. The feelings inside her were impossible to explain to a human brain, she realized, but they were there.

Completion. Elation. A knowing. Like this really was the one and only. There could never be another male of any species that would make her heart ache with joy and love like Vaidd did.

But the human memories that still dwelled within were confused and wary. They didn't understand this newfound passion, didn't comprehend how she could love someone she'd just met so fully and completely. Like she'd die without him near her.

"What are you thinking?" he murmured, his gaze coming up to meet hers.

Dot blew out a breath. How could she explain this? "I hardly know you," she muttered. "I just don't understand why I'm feeling like I am."

One side of his mouth slowly lifted into a mischievous grin. God, he was handsome. Everything she'd ever asked for in a man but never thought she'd have. "'Tis my wicked big cock."

Or almost everything, she thought on a grunt. "I'm being serious."

"I know." He sighed, the universal sound of a man who didn't feel like exploring the how and the why, just accepting things as is. But, to his credit, he explored them with her anyway. "The longer we are together, the more you will understand. 'Tis no way for me to explain it, *zya*. Not really."

That she could believe. "Do you feel confused too?"

"Nay."

"Why not?"

He shrugged. "I've grown up this way my entire life. I've got nothing to look back on and compare it against." He didn't smile, he rarely did that, but his eyes were on fire. "You are my one, my only," he murmured. "There could never be another for me."

That did things to her heart she couldn't begin to describe. How a spinster like her could end up with a gorgeous man like this—who wanted only her no less!—was beyond wonderful. And better yet, she felt the same way about him.

"I feel the same way," she said on a soft smile. "And yet the confusion remains."

"One day there will be no confusion. One day all parts of your mind will accept what is true."

That sounded so arrogant. And yet she knew he was right. What's more, it's exactly what she needed to hear.

"Lay thy head down upon me, *vorah*," Vaidd commanded, yawning. When she complied, he squeezed her affectionately. "We've six entire lives together. All will be well. On the morrow we can talk more of this."

"Six lives?" she said excitedly, her head bobbing up. "But how can—"

He grunted as he placed a gentle finger to her lips. "Verily, the god of speech did not overlook you when handing out things to say."

She frowned. He grinned.

Dot's heart sped up. He had a beautiful smile.

"On the morrow then," she said, imitating his words. She loved the way it made her sound all British! "We can talk then."

* * * * *

Vaidd awoke to the feel of his Bloodmate licking his stiff cock. He sucked in a breath, his stomach muscles clenching, as he watched her go down on him. Her eyes were closed, a dreamy smile on her face, as she nigh unto suckled him blind.

He swallowed heavily. The stories of primitive females were true. Native Khan-Gori females would never think to do such a thing in so far as he was aware. Only the female yenni would suckle a Barbarian.

Catching her hair and holding it away from her face so as not to impede his view, Vaidd's eyelids grew heavy as he watched Dot's warm, suctioning mouth work up and down the length of his manhood. She sucked on him slowly, savoring him as though his cock was a favorite treat.

His balls were so tight they felt ready to explode.

"That's it," he said hoarsely, "love me with your mouth, little one." His toes curled as he watched her take him in, the sound of saliva meeting hard flesh further arousing him.

"Mmmm," Vaidd purred, lying back on an elbow. He guided her head with his hand, indicating he wanted suckled faster.

Dot met his challenge, fulfilled his desire. She sucked on his cock faster, her head bobbing up and down with the effort.

Vaidd hissed out his pleasure, his balls getting impossibly tighter. His jaw clenched and his teeth gritted as he watched his wife suck him off, suctioning his cock into her throat over and over, again and again.

"*Dot.*"

He burst on a loud growl that resonated throughout their lair. His cum spurted up, and she was quick to drink of him. Dot lapped at him with more proficiency than any female yenni, even sucking the hole at the tip to make sure not a single drop of his essence had been missed.

His breathing was labored as her head slowly came up. An eyebrow rose at the devilish look on her face. "Aye?" he panted.

She licked her lips, making him gulp. Never had he seen a woman of any species so sexy as this one. "Now that I've got you just like I want you..." Dot tantalizingly climbed up on his chest and stretched her gorgeous body out on him. "I've got a few questions that the speech god gave me to ask you."

Vaidd threw his head back and laughed. A twinkle in his eye, he grabbed both well-rounded cheeks on her backside and kneaded them like the treasures they were. "Ask away. I would never wish to displease the speech god."

Epilogue

Vaidd had answered all of Dot's questions that morning in their lair. And oh boy had she had quite a few! She smiled at the memory as she sat on the floor with her first litter—a son and two daughters—and taught the adorable three-year-old pups how to shape-shift.

"*Vazi*," her daughter, Nitara, inquired. Nitara had been named for Vaidd's favored sister. "When will papa be home?"

"Aye, when, *vazi*?" her two other pups chirped in.

Dot smiled, unadulterated happiness enveloping her every single time one of her babies called her *vazi*—mommy. She sometimes had to pinch herself to remind her human memories that this wasn't all a dream.

Vaidd, she conceded, had been right when he'd told her that one day her mind would fully accept the truth for what it was. It hadn't taken long. Maybe—oh...a whole day!

"He'll be home soon," she promised. He'd only been gone an hour, long enough to go barter for some of her favorite candies from the local merchant. He planned to trade two female yenni for a six-months supply. Why? She was pregnant again and Vaidd had found during the first litter that the candies in question were her favorites. "Now don't you want to surprise papa by showing off how good you are at shape-shifting?"

Nitara popped the thumb out of her mouth. "Nay." Her piece spoken, she popped it back in. Dot could only giggle.

By the time Vaidd returned, his pups were ready to pounce, and pounce they did. Dot stayed on the floor, smiling as she watched her Bloodmate play with them, wondering why it was that human bonds never fully developed to the extent that Khan-Gori ones did. The babies couldn't stand for *either* parent to be out of their sight. Usually human children preferred one parent's presence to the other.

Khan-Gor, as it turned out, was a pretty fascinating place to live. A medieval realm in some ways—especially in terms of fashion and how the caved cities and marketplaces looked. A primitive realm in other ways—especially in terms of the whole drinking each other's blood and hunting dinner for yourself thing. And a technologically advanced realm in yet other ways—especially in terms of the weaponry and space-traveling ships that could be found here. Khan-Gor was yin and yang, ancient and advanced, modern and a throwback.

It was perfection.

Well, Dorothy, there's no place like home…

This *was* her home, the large cave-lair that boasted thirty chambers, a vast dining hall, and a world of comfort. This *was* her family, the babies and husband that she loved so much. She couldn't imagine life without them, and didn't want to either.

Later, after the pups had been fed and put to bed, Vaidd turned to Dot with those smoldering, blazing eyes of his. She rose to her feet and held her arms up to the giant. He picked her up so she could wrap her arms around his neck and kiss him like he'd never been kissed before.

"I love you," she whispered against his mouth.

He gave her an affectionate squeeze. "And I love you, my little one."

Their tongues danced and dueled, and before long Vaidd was hard as a rock. Dot purred into his mouth, rubbing her pussy against his erection. Not one to miss a mating moment, her Bloodmate carried her to their bedchamber and laid her on the soft animal hides so that he could love her properly.

"You have that devilish twinkle in your eyes, my love," Vaidd murmured as he settled himself on top of her.

She grinned. That's because she loved sex. Lots and lots of sweaty, pumping, pounding, gloriously wicked, undeniably naughty, kinky as all hell S-E-X with a capital S for *Sex*. And, she conceded, because she loved him and would be forever grateful to whatever power brought her to this place. Oh and there was one other reason for the devilish twinkle in her eyes, too...

"Well," she said in her Marilyn Monroe whisper, "I was thinking we could get a little kinky tonight."

Vaidd grunted. He slashed a definitive hand through the air. "Nay. There will be no shoving one of those toys of yours up my arse this eve." He sniffed. "I'm not in the mood. Leastways, not now."

Dot chuckled. He loved her latest invention, "Annie-In-My-Arse", and he damn well knew it. Annie had developed quite a few devoted fans in the merchant stalls for a reason. Dot was certain her husband would be in the mood before long. But for now...

"I love you," Dot breathed out as Vaidd sank into her welcoming, tight flesh. Oh how she loved him!

"I love you, too, *zya*," Vaidd whispered between kisses to her neck. He lifted his head and smiled. "Now and forever, you are my one and only." His sexy, light brown eyebrows rose. "Even if you do like putting wicked toys up your Bloodmate's arse."

About the author:

Jaid Black is a novelist for Ellora's Cave and, most recently, Berkley/Jove. Her earlier (steamy but not erotic) titles can be found under the pen name Tia Isabella. A single mother, Jaid and the kids enjoy traveling together as time allows. When Jaid gets her way, which usually involves a lot of begging and dire threats, they head toward Europe. When the kids get their way, which is usually the case, they head for Disney World.

In addition to writing erotic romances, Jaid also collaborates on horror novels and screenplays (horror and romantic comedies) with fellow EC author Claudia Rose. Their joint pen name is Millar Black.

Jaid welcomes mail from readers. You can write to her c/o Ellora's Cave Publishing at 1337 Commerce Drive, Suite 13, Stow OH 44224.

Also by Jaid Black:

Warlord

God Of Fire

The Possession*

Sins of the Father

Tremors

The Obsession

Vanished

_Death Row: The Trilogy_*

The Fugitive

The Hunter

The Avenger

Politically Incorrect Tale:

Stalked

Trek Mi Q'an:

Empress' New Clothes*

Seized*

No Mercy*

Enslaved*

No Escape♦

No Fear♦

Dementia*

Anthologies

The Hunted*

Enchained*

* in print

♦ print book _Conquest_

Why an electronic book?

We live in the Information Age — an exciting time in the history of human civilization in which technology rules supreme and continues to progress in leaps and bounds every minute of every hour of every day. For a multitude of reasons, more and more avid literary fans are opting to purchase e-books instead of paperbacks. The question to those not yet initiated to the world of electronic reading is simply: *why?*

1. *Price.* An electronic title at Ellora's Cave Publishing runs anywhere from 40-75% less than the cover price of the <u>exact same title</u> in paperback format. Why? Cold mathematics. It is less expensive to publish an e-book than it is to publish a paperback, so the savings are passed along to the consumer.

2. *Space.* Running out of room to house your paperback books? That is one worry you will never have with electronic novels. For a low one-time cost, you can purchase a handheld computer designed specifically for e-reading purposes. Many e-readers are larger than the average handheld, giving you plenty of screen room. Better yet, hundreds of titles can be stored within your new library — a single

microchip. (Please note that Ellora's Cave does not endorse any specific brands. You can check our website at www.ellorascave.com for customer recommendations we make available to new consumers.)

3. *Mobility.* Because your new library now consists of only a microchip, your entire cache of books can be taken with you wherever you go.

4. *Personal preferences are accounted for.* Are the words you are currently reading too small? Too large? Too...**ANNOYING**? Paperback books cannot be modified according to personal preferences, but e-books can.

5. *Innovation.* The way you read a book is not the only advancement the Information Age has gifted the literary community with. There is also the factor of what you can read. Ellora's Cave Publishing will be introducing a new line of interactive titles that are available in e-book format only.

6. *Instant gratification.* Is it the middle of the night and all the bookstores are closed? Are you tired of waiting days—sometimes weeks—for online and offline bookstores to ship the novels you bought? Ellora's Cave Publishing sells instantaneous downloads 24 hours a day, 7 days a week, 365 days a year. Our e-book delivery system is 100% automated, meaning your order is filled as soon as you pay for it.

Those are a few of the top reasons why electronic novels are displacing paperbacks for many an avid reader. As always, Ellora's Cave Publishing welcomes your questions and comments. We invite you to email us at service@ellorascave.com or write to us directly at: 1337 Commerce Drive, Suite 13, Stow OH 4424.

Printed in the United States
53965LVS00001B/328-369